SAXBY
SCHOOLBOY DETECTIVE
SMART

The *Saxby Smart – Schoolboy Detective*
series:

Find fun features, exclusive mysteries
and much more at:
**www.saxbysmart.co.uk**

Find out more at:
**www.simoncheshire.co.uk**

## THE **POISONED ARROW**

# SIMON CHESHIRE

*Piccadilly*

*To Brenda, Ruth, Melissa, Vivien, Mary, Becky, Hilary*
*and all the rest of the gang, without whom*
*this production would not have been possible . . .*

First published in Great Britain in 2009
by Piccadilly Press,
A Templar/Bonnier publishing company
Deepdene Lodge, Deepdene Avenue,
Dorking, Surrey, RH5 4AT
www.piccadillypress.co.uk

Text copyright © Simon Cheshire, 2009

A catalogue record for this book is available
from the British Library

ISBN: 978 1 84812 037 2 (paperback)

3 5 7 9 10 8 6 4 2

Printed in the UK by CPI Group (UK) Ltd, Croydon, CR0 4YY

# Introduction:
# Important Facts

My name is Saxby Smart and I'm a private detective. I go to St Egbert's School, my office is in the garden shed, and this is a collection of my case files. Unlike some detectives, I don't have a sidekick, so that part I'm leaving up to you – pay attention, I'll ask questions.

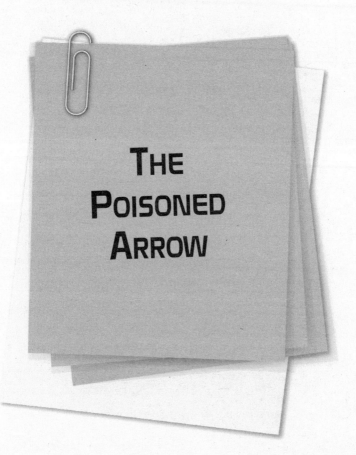

# THE
# POISONED
# ARROW

# CHAPTER ONE

SOMETIMES, BEING A BRILLIANT SCHOOLBOY detective – as I am – can have its moments of danger. Not very many, thank goodness, but it happens now and again.

Looking back through my case files, there have been several times when I've been placed in a situation of real, actual, genuine peril. For example, I narrowly avoided falling flat on my face while chasing the villains in their getaway lorry during the case of *The Bloodsucker's Grave*. And I was very nearly pushed into a huge tank full of cow poo during *The Mystery of Eviltree Farm*. However, only twice have I ever faced a situation which could truthfully be described as 'Oh-no-get-outta-there-*now*'.

The case of *The Poisoned Arrow* is perhaps the most hair-raising example.

5

It was 8.45 p.m. on a Friday evening. A sweeping fog dampened the distant glow of the streetlights. The cloudy, moonless sky cast a darkness over everything that was so deep I kept feeling as if I was staring into a bottomless pit.

I was standing, alone, on the gravelly forecourt outside the Rackham Road Community Theatre. This theatre, which is situated on the edge of town and which doubles up as a venue for all kinds of local events, is a rather squat, lumpy building, which looks like it's been put together using giant toy blocks instead of bricks. Most people call it the 'Turtle-Shell'. I was standing close to the hideous statue that's plonked down outside it, the one which shows four human figures striking dramatic poses. I guess it's meant to be theatrical.

I was looking for my phone. I'd realised I'd dropped it out there on the gravel somewhere, and it was vital that I retrieved it immediately. I was expecting a very important call, a call that would signal the endgame of a particularly nasty crime.

In the misty darkness, the crunch of my shoes on the gravel sounded like mountains collapsing. I glanced around nervously. The cold eeriness of the evening set me thinking about one or two creepy movies I should never have watched. The fog was thickening. The theatre's full-to-bursting parking area was only fifty metres away, but I could barely make it out. The streetlights on Rackham Road seemed to have become dimmer.

Where was that blasted phone?

Right by my feet, as it turned out! I glanced down, and there it was. Tutting to myself, I bent down and scooped it up. Good – I hadn't missed any calls.

I was about to turn and hurry back inside the theatre, when the sound of approaching footsteps froze me to the spot. Pocketing my phone, I stood up and stared uneasily into the surrounding gloom. I could feel my heart beginning to thump.

Then suddenly, out of the darkness, emerging through the mist came four, five, no six hulking figures – tall, heavy men, all of them smothered in dark coats. They were each wearing a horrible Halloween pumpkin mask.

I think my heart actually stopped for a few seconds. The crime I'd been expecting was about to take place!

The men marched towards the building, quickly but calmly. The darkness of the theatre's unlit forecourt was keeping me out of their sight, but I'd be spotted in a matter of seconds. I had to get away! If they saw me . . .

The heftiest of the men, out in front, was carrying a large canvas bag. It was clearly heavy. Knowing what was about to happen, I realised with horror that inside the bag must be weapons of some kind.

I couldn't risk being seen! But if I took a single step, the crunch of the gravel would instantly alert them.

I have never, ever, *ever* been so scared in all my life. It felt as if my insides had been forced through a paper shredder.

What could I *do*?

At that moment, my phone trilled. Loudly.

The man in front halted. 'Is someone there?' he boomed. 'Show yourself! Now!'

He twitched an arm to usher the others forward.

I didn't dare breathe. The only thought going through my head was: Why do I let myself get into these messes?

# Chapter Two

OK, HERE'S THE FLASHBACK. HOP back in time a few days. Imagine everything's suddenly gone zzzip in reverse, until we arrive at the previous Monday afternoon, about five o'clock. I was in my garden shed – or rather, my Crime Headquarters, as I prefer to call it.

I'd spent about an hour shoving at the gardening and DIY stuff I'm forced to share the shed with. It had been teetering, in a giant wobbly mound, across my desk and filing cabinet. I'd managed to crush it back a bit, so that at least it wasn't in imminent danger of all falling on top of me.

I sat in my Thinking Chair, the battered old red leather armchair where I do all my detective-style pondering. I was sorting through some of the case notes

9

from my filing cabinet, a stack of papers spread across my knees. I was also keeping half a narrowed eye on that giant wobbly mound of DIY stuff. I was sure those empty paint tins were just waiting for a chance to clatter down on top of me the minute I wasn't looking.

At that moment, I heard a new case approaching. The sound of someone doing vocal exercises drifted into the shed. A load of 'la-la-la-laaaa's and 'me-me-me-meeee's and random lines from well-known stage musicals were being sung at maximum volume. From the way the sound was bouncing around, I judged that the singer was turning the corner at the end of my street and walking this way.

How did I know this was a new case coming my way, and not just somebody down the street having a singsong? Two reasons: Firstly, it was the voice of someone about my age, and since there are surprisingly few other kids of any age in my street (none of whom ever sing in public!), I guessed that this particular kid was probably heading my way. Secondly, there was only one person I knew who'd be la-ing and me-ing all over the place like that: Tom Bland, the gangly, swirly-blond-haired boy from my school and the case of *The Stranger in the Mirror*.

I wouldn't have called him a friend of mine, as such, but everyone at St Egbert's School knew Tom Bland. He was rather snobby and rather self-centred, and totally set on being the world's greatest actor when he grew up. He could be a right prima donna, too. Oh yes, everyone at St Egbert's was familiar with Tom Bland.

It was highly unlikely that he'd be heading this way on a purely social visit. If Tom Bland was coming to see me, it was pretty certain that he was in need of my detective services again!

A few moments later, there was a sharp knock at my shed door. 'Come in, Tom!' I called.

The door opened and Tom bounced in. 'How did you know it was me?' he gasped.

'Just a lucky guess,' I said, shrugging. 'What's the problem? How can I help you?'

He started pacing about the floor of the shed. Not an easy thing to do in a shed with so little space.

'Catastrophe!' he cried. 'Calamity! Ruin! Disaster stares me in the face at this very moment! Er, not meaning you, Saxby . . .'

'No, understood,' I said.

'I don't mean *you're* a disaster or anything,' he burbled.

'No, understood,' I said. 'Calm down. Start at the beginning. Give me some background information.'

I hoisted the heap of case notes off my knees and on to the desk. I offered Tom my Thinking Chair. He sank into it, striking a pose like a troubled soul in a Victorian painting, the back of his hand brushing at his forehead.

'You're right,' he said. 'I must give you the facts of the case. That's the vital thing with detectives, isn't it, making sure you give them the facts of the case?'

'Quite right,' I said encouragingly.

He took a deep breath and his hands took long symmetrical scoops out of the air in a deliberate I-am-calm gesture. He spoke as if addressing an audience of eager, wide-eyed fans.

'As you know, Saxby, I'm someone with a great interest in the world of the theatre.'

'Yes, I'd spotted that,' I said quietly.

He nodded. 'And as part of my preparations for my long-term career in the acting profession, I'm heavily involved in the Rackham Road Amateur Dramatic Society. It's mostly for adults, I'm the only regular under-sixteen member.'

'Is that the one which puts on plays at that weird-looking building? Whassitcalled, the Turtle-Shell?'

'That's the one, yes. We presented a splendid production of Shakespeare's *Much Ado About Nothing* last year. I was terrific in it. Of course, it's amazing I managed to combine my appearances at Rackham Road with my work on the school play. It's a wonder I didn't collapse from sheer exhaustion, but no doubt —'

'A-hem, the facts of the case . . .' I prompted.

'Oh, yes, sorry,' he said. 'Anyway, we're currently staging a production of *The Poisoned Arrow*. Do you know it?'

'Nope.'

'It's an action-packed historical drama, set in the Middle Ages. Lots of sword fights and shocked facial expressions – it's very good. I play Wilbert, a poor peasant boy who overcomes enormous odds to gain the throne of the kingdom, when the villainous landowner Baron Thornicroft tries to —'

He glanced at me. I was frowning.

'Facts of the case, right,' he said. 'Are you sure you don't know *The Poisoned Arrow*? It did really well in the West End of London a couple of years ago.'

'Nope,' I said.

'Hmm. Anyway, we're doing this play. And the production is hugely, gigantically, vastly important for all of us at Rackham Road, for three reasons. Reason one: we're only doing one perfomance, and it's for charity. Our theatre runs on donations and voluntary help and it's always been short of money. But now debts have mounted up and we need a pile of cash to stop the place from being demolished. If we go bust, the place gets sold to some money-mad corporation and turned into flats. Reason two: because it's for charity, we've got none other than the marvellous Sir Gilbert Smudge himself playing King Lionel. Reason three: because it's for charity, and because a professional actor as famous as Sir Gilbert is involved, the audience is going to be filled with every important person for miles around. The mayor, lots of local business people, three Members of Parliament . . . all sorts of influential types. There's a long and very impressive guest list. Sir Gilbert's even got some of his old celebrity pals coming up from London. There'll be bow ties, dinner jackets, ladies dripping with pearl necklaces, the works.'

'Wow,' I said. 'Sounds like it'll be quite an event. Even I've heard of Gilbert Smudge. He's in all those old movies and TV series that keep getting shown on ITV3, right?'

'Oh yes,' said Tom, bright-eyed with enthusiasm, 'he's had a very distinguished career. He's won every award going. Marvellous actor. Nice man, too. Full of interesting theatrical stories. Got an odd smell of paint about him, though, can't quite work that one out. But a marvellous actor.'

'So, umm, at the risk of sounding a bit rude,' I said, 'if he's so very famous and distinguished, why is he appearing with the Rackham Road Amateur Dramatic Society? Charity performance or not, that's an odd thing to find someone like him doing, isn't it?'

Tom squirmed slightly in the armchair. His face wriggled with embarrassment. 'Yes, well,' he said at last, 'times have been a little hard for him recently. He's not as young as he was, as my granny would say. Offers of acting roles have been rather thin on the ground for him, and some of the parts he's accepted in the last few years haven't always been a wise move. He should never have agreed to play Mr Squitty in that *Masked Avenger* movie. It dented his reputation as a serious actor. Then he was a giant rabbit in *The Happy Bunnybears II: Bobo's Journey*, and since then the work has dried up almost completely. Sad, very sad. Marvellous actor. I think this performance is something of a last chance for him. He's hoping it will get him some good reviews and lead to better things. We've got quite a few media people coming. Newspapers, radio and so on.'

'So I assume the perfomance is going to be very exclusive?' I said. 'Eye-poppingly expensive tickets, that sort of thing?'

'Ah, no,' said Tom, wagging a finger. 'Sir Gilbert suggested a different idea, based on something he did for one of those TV charity nights about ten years ago. The tickets are only a few pounds each, and the people on the guest list are getting in for nothing.'

'So where does the fund-raising come in?' I asked.

'During the interval, Sir Gilbert is going to give the

15

audience a please-give-generously speech, then go around collecting donations personally. The guests are expecting it – the details are all printed on the back of the tickets.'

'I get it,' I said, smiling. 'With all those influential people there – most of them pretty wealthy – he's likely to collect a small fortune. They'll probably start competing to be thought of as the most generous. Especially once the media start taking pictures. Clever.'

'Exactly,' said Tom with a grin. 'Everyone wins. The posh folk get to look important, Sir Gilbert makes a triumphant comeback, the Turtle-Shell is saved from the bulldozers, and the Rackham Road Amateur Dramatics Society scores the biggest hit in its history.'

'I must say,' I said, 'it's all looking very impressive.' I paused for a moment. 'So, what's this calamity you were on about? What's happened?'

Tom slumped back in the Thinking Chair, looking all pale and feeble. 'It's a nightmare,' he whispered. 'A living nightmare. The whole event is threatened!'

'Let me guess,' I said. 'Ummmm, someone has broken into the building during the night and stolen all the costumes?'

'No,' said Tom.

'The sets have been sabotaged?'

'No.'

16

'Sir Gilbert Smudge has been kidnapped and held to ransom?'

'No.'

'OK, so what crime *has* been committed?' I asked.

'None,' said Tom. 'None at all.'

I gave Tom the same narrow-eyed look I'd been giving that teetering pile of paint pots in the corner. 'So . . . why are you here? What's the calamity?'

'Oh, there's *going* to be a crime,' said Tom. 'I can feel it in me bones, as my grandad would say. On Friday night, *The Poisoned Arrow* is going to be turned into a major disaster by evil forces as yet unidentified.'

If I'd narrowed my eyes any more, I'd have been unable to see. 'Let me get this straight,' I said. 'You want me to investigate a crime which *hasn't been committed*?'

# CHAPTER
# Three

'YET,' CORRECTED TOM. 'HASN'T BEEN committed *yet*. That's why I need your help. You must identify the evil forces at work and stop them.'

I let out a long, slow breath and pressed my knuckles to my eyes like you see them do in gritty police dramas on TV. 'You want me to unmask someone who hasn't actually done anything wrong yet?'

'That's about it, yes,' said Tom.

'You want me to go after an *innocent* person?' I cried.

'They won't be innocent after Friday,' protested Tom. 'They're out to ruin the performance!'

I wasn't sure whether to let out an almighty scream or just curl up and whimper quietly for a while. 'I can't even *begin* to list the things that are wrong with that idea,' I muttered. I suddenly felt as if I was trapped in one of those science fiction stories in which someone gets arrested for murdering their great-great-grandmother twenty years before they were born.

'I've got evidence,' said Tom. 'I'm not imagining this whole thing, you know.'

'Ah,' I said. 'Evidence. OK. Give me your evidence.'

Tom leaned forward on my Thinking Chair. He glanced sideways, as if he expected to find half a dozen villains in black eye masks looming over his shoulder.

'The play's director, Morag Wellington-Barnes, is acting *very* suspiciously.' He nodded slowly, wide-eyed, as if he'd just demonstrated the answer to a stunningly difficult maths problem.

I sighed. 'Tom, that's not evidence. That's just you.'

'She's up to something,' said Tom. 'She's been one of us Rackham Roaders for years, since before I joined, so I know her quite well. She's gone very odd. Even odder than usual. She keeps losing her temper, biting her nails – revolting habit – and staring off into nowhere with a vacant expression on her face.'

'Surely she's just nervous?' I said. 'There's every reason to be.'

'You won't say that when you meet her,' said Tom. His nostrils flared into a semi-sneer. 'I know I'm thought of as arrogant at school, it's no use protesting . . .'

(He was right. I wasn't about to.)

'. . . I simply have high standards,' said Tom loftily, 'but Morag Wellington-Barnes is more fearsome than a sergeant major in a platoon full of marines. However, she's very good at organising plays, so everyone puts up with her. Obviously, whenever I'm involved in a play, I'm always coming up with superb ideas for improvements to scenes. She rarely listens to me at the best of times but at the moment she's making one crackpot decision after another and nobody can change her mind.'

'What sort of crackpot decisions?' I asked.

'Well, she's reduced the cast, for one thing,' said Tom. '*The Poisoned Arrow* has nineteen speaking parts – it's quite a large-scale production – but she's cut out eight of them. All the minor roles have simply been taken out. Madness! I feel sorry for Mrs Smoth – she was looking forward to playing Cackling Old Crone in scene six and now she's out. She's ninety-six, you know.'

'Maybe Morag thought the play was too long or something?' I shrugged.

'Rubbish!' cried Tom. 'This play was a huge hit in London. Solid drama and excitement from beginning to end. If anything, it's not long *enough*! And as well as that, Morag's ruined the play's whole staging. She's scrapped all the lighting effects. Insanity! She's insisting that the whole performance is done with the house lights up!'

'The what-lights?' I asked.

'House lights,' repeated Tom. 'The lights where the audience sits. The ones that normally go out in a theatre or cinema when the performance starts, those are called the house lights. Morag is insisting they're left on, right the way through the play! The atmosphere will be ruined!'

'Hmm, well, yes, I guess that's unusual,' I said. 'But she *is* the director. Isn't that simply her approach to the play?'

'I told you,' said Tom, 'she's normally *good* at this sort of thing. Do these sound like good ideas to you?'

I shuffled uncomfortably. 'You're talking about, what'ya'callit, artistic differences. You say there's crime involved, but there's *no crime whatsoever* involved in what you've told me. And no, before you say it, a crime-against-the-theatre is *not* an actual crime!'

Tom shook his head. 'You misunderstand me. I really *do* think there's going to be an actual crime committed. A real, serious crime. Look, I have more evidence here.'

He pulled a couple of small sheets of folded-up paper from his pocket and handed them over to me. 'I found these backstage,' he said. 'Someone had obviously dropped them by mistake but I don't know who.'

Curious, I unfolded the first one. It was a plan of the

theatre. It showed the road at the front of the building and the large open field at the rear (which was part of a neighbouring farm). It also showed three ways of getting into the theatre – the main entrance at the front, and two emergency doors (one to each side of the audience seating area). A set of large double doors, in the unseen-from-the-audience area behind the stage, were shown to open out on to the field, but they were marked:

*These only open from inside. Their is no way in here.*

'Well,' I said, examining the sheets more closely, to see if there were any clues to be had from the paper itself, 'the only thing we can say for sure about this person is that they didn't pay attention during English lessons. *Their is no way* ought to be *There is no way*. This first paper was torn from an ordinary spiral-bound jotter pad. Nothing unusual, and no [*sniff!*], no sign of perfume or aftershave. From the way they're slightly crumpled and curved, I'd say they'd been carried in the back pocket of someone's trousers.'

I unfolded the other sheet. It was slightly larger than the first, a printed list of twenty-two names, none of which I recognised. Five of them had an asterisk marked against them, and all twenty-two were followed by a letter and a number.

'Are these people from the special guest list for Friday's performance?' I said.

'All of them.' Tom nodded. 'The whole list is about sixty names long. Why these twenty-two should have been picked out, I have no idea.' He pointed to the letters and numbers. 'You see that? Some sort of code. I've been trying to make sense of it, but it seems random. B4, then against the next name there's B28, then A2 . . . H16 . . . J7 . . . I31 . . . Can you work out what it means?'

A definite possibility crossed my mind. 'Since we know that all these people will be at the play on Friday night,' I said, 'then, yes, I think I've spotted what this code means.'

Have you spotted it too?

'I think this indicates the seats they'll be sitting in,' I said. 'Row B, Seat 4, and so on.'

'Ooh, of course!' groaned Tom. 'I should have realised.'

'However,' I said, 'if these are seat numbers, then you've got a strange seating plan. These people must be dotted about all over the theatre. Aren't you seating all your special guests at the front?'

Tom almost sprang out of the chair. 'That's another of Morag's crackpot decisions,' he cried. 'I heard her and Sir Gilbert talking about it the other day. The guests *had* been allocated the seats at the front, but then Morag changed it. He was asking her why one of his friends had been plonked over by the toilets. She just got snotty with him and told him her decision was final. Mad!'

Then he almost sprang out of the chair again. 'There! That settles it! This is evidence! Morag must have made that list!'

'No,' I said patiently, 'it *isn't* evidence, and *anyone* could have made this list. The seating plan is hardly a secret, is it?'

'Hmm. No.'

'I still don't see any connection with any actual *crime*,' I continued.

'You won't be saying that in a minute!' said Tom. 'The other day, after rehearsals, I was putting the costumes away so I was a few minutes late leaving the theatre. As

I did so, I spotted Morag on the other side of the theatre's car park. She was deep in conversation with a brutish-looking man, standing beside a shiny black Mercedes.'

'Brutish-looking?'

'He was built like a boulder and bald as one too. Even at a distance of about a hundred metres, I could see that half his nose was missing. And he had a huge scar down one cheek. He also had a bodyguard in dark glasses standing behind him and the bodyguard was built like three boulders stuck on top of each other! I've never seen such an obvious villain!'

'Believe me, Tom,' I scoffed, 'there's no such thing as an obvious villain. Don't judge by appearances.'

'I've played many a villain on the stage,' said Tom loftily, 'so I know what I'm talking about. That man was a villain.'

I was about to remind him that real-life bad guys aren't quite the same as the ones in TV cartoons, but then I thought of something more important to say.

'Could you hear what they were talking about?'

'Not from that distance, no. But I'm sure it was something relating to the theatre. Both of them kept looking over at it.'

'Well, sorry, Tom,' I said, puzzled. 'I *still* don't see any connection with any actual crime. What conclusion does all this point to?'

'Oh, come on,' scoffed Tom, 'you're the detective. Think about what's happening on Friday evening. Add that to all the suspicious stuff I've told you about. Can't you see the obvious possibility?'

Suddenly, I could. A cold feeling slimed up my spine. Can you see what crime Tom was predicting?

'How many people are going to be in the theatre in total?' I gasped.

'Well, sixty-ish invited guests, plus anyone else who's bought a ticket,' said Tom. 'The place seats over five hundred in all and because Sir Gilbert's appearing, it's a sell-out.'

The cold feeling slimed up my spine all over again.

'Someone could rob that entire theatre audience,' I muttered in horror. 'Turn up with a few heavies, block the exits. On Friday, that place will contain hundreds of people and they're all going to have money with them. Ladies dripping with pearl necklaces, you said. They'll be sitting ducks. It'd be like an old fashioned stick-'em-up. Good grief, it'd be a mass mugging!'

Tom went as pale as a slice of cheap bread. 'Disaster! Calamity! And Morag's up to her eyeballs in the whole despicable scheme! Do you think she's hired a local gang or got some bad guys in from somewhere else?'

'Wait, wait, wait!' I cried. 'Hang on, be sensible. We still can't be sure about *any* of this. All we've got are vague suspicions and theoretical possibilities.'

'But a robbery *is* a possibility,' said Tom, 'and you've got to admit these papers suggest that one *is* being planned.'

'Maybe,' I replied. 'Only maybe. You say it's evidence. Well, if it is, it's the thinnest evidence I've ever seen. But I ought to have a bit of a dig around. Just in case. Can you get me into your next rehearsal? We don't want to alert any villainous elements that might be around, so I could pretend to be interested in joining the Society, something like that?'

'No problem,' said Tom.

'Good,' I said decisively. 'Never fear, Saxby Smart is on the case.'

---

## A Page From My Notebook

(Scribbled under the covers, way after bedtime.)

I need to think about this carefully. From all that Tom has told me, a robbery IS a possibility . . .

**BUT!** Just because it's POSSIBLE doesn't mean it WILL happen - doesn't even mean it MIGHT happen. We could simply be seeing a danger that ISN'T THERE AT ALL!

**BUT!** The decisions made by Morag the director COULD be interpreted in a sinister way:

• Her decision to cut down the number of people in the play COULD be an attempt to reduce the number of people who'd be backstage when the robbers turn up, thereby reducing the chances that someone, out of sight, might phone for help.

• Her decision to keep the house lights on COULD be a way to make it easier for the robbers to control the audience and spot anyone trying to escape.

• Her decision to place the guests all over the theatre COULD be a method to help the gang get to the wealthiest people quickly - gangster one takes this section of the audience, gangster two takes that section, and so on.

**ON THE OTHER HAND, PART 1:** Tom said that it was Sir Gilbert Smudge, the actor, who suggested the whole bring-along-your-money fund-raising idea in the first place. Could this mean that HE is the one who's hatching a plot?

**ON THE OTHER HAND, PART 2:** We have no idea WHO drew that plan or printed that list. Tom only thinks it was Morag because he already suspects her of being up to something. Those papers could belong to anyone. And if they DON'T belong to Morag, then any suspicions of her start to look weaker . . .

. . . Unless several people involved in the production are part of a plot?

. . . Or am I jumping to conclusions? Are Tom's suspicions totally unfounded, as I thought at first?

**BIG QUESTION:** WHO was the man with the scar? IS he involved? WAS Tom right to be alarmed? Or does the man have nothing to do with this business? What if he's just Morag's accountant or something like that? (Don't forget: just because someone LOOKS villainous, doesn't mean they are. I must stay fair and impartial!)

**VITALLY IMPORTANT POINT:** Where's the MOTIVE? (Beyond running off with a load of money, I mean!)

WHY would someone involved in the play want to wreck it? I need to concentrate on MOTIVE in my investigations . . .

I also need to get some sleep. Nighty night.

# CHAPTER Four

IN THE TWENTY-FIRST CENTURY, the old-fashioned, stick-'em-up bank robbery has become almost impossible. Security technology has become so good that the would-be thief has very little chance of getting away with anything like that any more.

So villains – serious, organised villains, I mean, not the grab-something-by-chance type – are becoming sneakier. Why not apply the principle of the traditional bank raid to new targets? Theatres, cinemas, offices, anywhere people might gather in numbers. A raid on *The Poisoned Arrow* would end up looting cash, phones, jewellery, whatever people happened to have with them.

Disturbing thoughts like this kept spinning around in my mind from the moment I woke up the following day.

And the more they kept on spinning, the more worried I became. I began to understand why Tom had such an uneasy feeling about Friday's performance.

The morning's lessons were as painfully slow as an earwig pushing a brick up a hill. The voice of Mrs Penzler, our form teacher, seemed to slide into one long, droning sound, like the distant honking of a ship's horn.

At last it was lunch break and after collecting a tray of something that looked like it had already been eaten a couple of times ('It's vegetable stew,' whispered the kid next to me in the queue, and 'Ohhh,' I whispered back), I went to sit down next to my great friend Isobel 'Izzy' Moustique.

She was unwrapping the sandwiches in her packed lunch and flipping through a magazine. Izzy is St Egbert's School's number one Brain, as well as being the girliest girl you're ever likely to meet. If it's information you need, head straight for Izzy.

'No,' she said, glancing up from her magazine.

'I haven't said anything yet,' I cried.

'You don't need to,' she said, turning a page. 'You've got that look on your face, Saxby.'

'What look?' I said, innocently.

'That look which says, "I'm stuck on a case and I need your help again",' she told me, trying to squash down a smile.

32

'Am I really that predictable?' I mumbled. 'Am I really so transparent and easy-to-read? Does my face really betray my every innermost thought?'

'Yes,' replied Izzy.

'Oh. Well, anyway, I'm stuck on a case and I need your help again.'

'No,' she said. 'Sorry, I've got a load of science homework to finish. And so have you, come to think of it! We'll both be in trouble if it doesn't get done.'

We chatted about school stuff for a minute or two, while I sniffed cautiously at the vegetable stew. I took the two pieces of paper Tom had given me out of my pocket and looked over them again.

'What are those?' asked Izzy.

'Oh, nothing really,' I said with a shrug. 'Just possible clues leading to a serious crime which might engulf around five hundred people at the end of this week. Anyway, we're both busy, as you say, so, er, I'll see what I can find out for myself. Not a problem.'

I guessed it would be roughly thirty seconds before Izzy's curiosity got the better of her. Twenty-six seconds later, after she'd glanced at the papers eight times, she finally blurted, 'OK, what do you need to know?'

I told her about Tom's visit to my shed. Then I handed her the mysterious list of names.

'What I'm particularly interested to know,' I said, 'is

33

why these twenty-two names should be on a separate list like this, and also what the asterisks against these five names might signify. Don't worry about those letter-and-number codes, because I've worked out —'

'They're just seat numbers, obviously,' said Izzy, examining the list.

'Er, right, yeah,' I said hurriedly. I finished the rest of my stew. It tasted better than it looked.

The bell went for afternoon lessons. Izzy pocketed the list and stood up.

'If I'm late handing in my science homework,' she said with mock annoyance, 'I'm going to blame you.'

'I knew you'd give in,' I said, grinning. 'I can read you like a book.'

Once school was finished for the day, I caught up with Tom and we headed over to Rackham Road. Tom talked about the play – and about how brilliant he was in it – *non-stop* from the moment we left the school gates. By the time we arrived at the Turtle-Shell, my brain was beginning to boggle at the way one human mouth could produce so many words in so short a time.

We entered the odd-looking building through the main entrance. Inside was a wide foyer, and beyond that was the impressively large and rather cavernous auditorium. Its sides were lined with curtains, one or two of which were drawn back to reveal floor-to-ceiling windows which let in the last of the afternoon sunlight. Ahead of us was the stage, on which a dozen or more adults were milling about.

'. . . so you can clash the swords together during the fights and they sound great, but they're not dangerous,' said Tom. He looked over at the stage. 'Ah! The cast are all here. Well, now I've arrived we can begin the rehearsal.'

I quickly stuffed the white headphones I'd just taken out of my ears into my pocket. 'Pardon?'

Tom blinked at me. 'Have you heard anything I've said?'

'Every word,' I lied. 'Fascinating. Don't forget, when you introduce me, my name is Raymond Chandler and I'm here because I'm studying *The Poisoned Arrow* for a national essay-writing competition.'

Tom tutted. He marched ahead, down the aisle between two blocks of seats and up to the edge of the stage.

'Afternoon everyone,' he called. 'This is my pal, Saxby. He's a fan of my acting so he's volunteered to be my Personal Assistant for the week. Here, take my school bag, Saxby, and fetch me a glass of water. Nice and cold, please.'

I sighed. Why are undercover identities always such a problem? The detectives on TV never seem to have this trouble.

A debate was going on amongst the actors. It carried on roughly as follows:

Stage 1 – Half the actors were saying that the big battle scene (which took up most of the second half of the play) needed something a bit more spectacular than everyone running around wielding swords. How about some horses? Horses would have taken part in a real medieval battle.

Stage 2 – The other half of the actors said that this was the most ridiculous idea they'd ever heard. You can't have horses clomping about on the stage!

Stage 3 – The first half of the actors said no, of course not real horses. But they could use pantomime horses! Someone had a friend who had three horse costumes, which could be borrowed for a tenner.

Stage 4 – The second half of the actors said hang on, no, wait, on second thought, *that* was the most ridiculous idea they'd ever heard. *The Poisoned Arrow* was a historical drama, not a pie-in-the-face comedy for toddlers!

And so on, and so on.

It won't surprise you to learn that Tom was firmly on the side of the second half of the actors. I kept well out of it.

Morag Wellington-Barnes also seemed to be keeping out of the argument. She was sitting with her legs dangling over the edge of the stage, tapping furiously at a laptop (in between nibbling at her fingernails). She was dressed in various shades of leather and suede and wore a pair of sunglasses which were very small, very round and very dark. I could see what Tom had meant about her. She looked like the sort of person who'd like to introduce prison sentences for anyone who drops biscuit crumbs on the carpet.

'Morag,' called one of the actors, 'what's your take on this? Are we going with the pantomime horses or not?'

Morag swung her gaze to one side and, even though her eyes were invisible behind those glasses, she speared the actor with a look which could have frozen volcanic lava.

'Would it involve using more actors?' she said, in a voice which could have turned lemonade to stone.

'Yes.'

'Then no,' she said. 'End of.'

She left her laptop glowing on a table that was part of a banquet scene. She gathered some of the actors in the middle of the stage and told them that the scene in which Baron Thornicroft plots the downfall of King Lionel was coming across as a load of old rubbish and that she wanted it done with far more anger and intensity. One or two of the actors' bottom lips started to wobble slightly. Tom was reading through his script and practising his dramatic facial expressions – surprise! Fear! Thoughtfulness!

Meanwhile, I was watching a figure sitting quietly on a chair towards one side of the stage. Sir Gilbert Smudge (I recognised him from all those old TV shows on ITV3) was also going over his script, his creased face and whiskery white beard held still in concentration.

He was wearing faded jeans, scuffed shoes and an old corduroy jacket that had been patched several times in different places. At first, I assumed he was simply one of those people who's happy being scruffy, but then I saw him search his pockets and come up with nothing but an old bus ticket and a scraggy paper tissue. His nose wrinkled up in dismay. After looking around for a few moments, wondering what to do, he caught the eye of one of the actors who'd been given an earful by Morag.

'Would you mind, old chap,' he said, in deep, mellow tones, 'advancing me a coin or two for the coffee machine? I seem to be temporarily without funds. Oh, many thanks, many thanks, much obliged to you.'

And off he wandered to a vending machine in the backstage area. Tom had told me that Sir Gilbert was having trouble finding acting jobs, but I'd only thought about that in terms of his acting career and reputation. It simply hadn't occurred to me until now that someone as well known as Sir Gilbert Smudge might barely have a penny to his name! He must have *had* money – he'd been in all those movies and TV series. He must have got through a lot of cash in the past. I felt very sorry for the guy.

Suddenly, something important occurred to me. I pulled out my notebook and re-read the notes I'd made in bed the previous night. From what I'd just observed, I now had a possible answer to a vitally important question.

Can you guess what was going through my mind?

If Sir Gilbert was penniless these days, could I have found a motive for the crime? Could he be in serious financial trouble? Could it be that Sir Gilbert's fund-raising idea was a cover for a larger, sinister plan?

Sir Gilbert wandered back on to the stage, sipping at a steaming paper cup. I found it hard to believe that this distinguished, friendly-looking but rather sad figure could be involved with a gang of villains. Then I reminded myself that some of the worst crooks I'd ever encountered had seemed equally innocent at first.

'We'll rehearse King Lionel's death scene,' announced Morag. 'Soldiers, I want more shock from you this time, please, it's your beloved king dying here, not a pet hamster. And Baron Thornicroft, ease up on the evil cackling.'

Everyone took their places. Sir Gilbert put his coffee down and stood centre stage, brandishing an imaginary sword. Tom, playing Wilbert the peasant boy, crouched beside him.

'Morag, m'dear,' said Sir Gilbert, 'do we know yet how many pouches of fake blood there'll be under my shirt for this scene?'

'Just the one, Sir Gilbert,' said Morag.

'*One?*' cried Tom in disgust. (Some of the actors groaned quietly. Tom's interruptions were obviously a regular thing here.) 'Is that all? He's getting a sword through his chest – we need buckets of it! Why can't we be realistic?'

'Because, Tom,' said Morag firmly, 'we're trying to entertain the audience, not make them vomit. OK, everyone, from the top.'

Tom huffed grumpily.

Morag, Sir Gilbert and everyone else concentrated on the scene. Which gave me an opportunity to concentrate on everything else. I sat in the front row of the auditorium, watching the goings-on carefully in case there were any clues to be spotted.

At that point, I spotted Morag's laptop. It was still sitting where she'd left it, its screen shining brightly. Even from a distance, I could see that she'd been writing an email.

I told myself that snooping at other people's emails was utterly, totally wrong. Then I told myself that planning a robbery was even worse and that a bit of snooping might be excusable under the circumstances.

I casually stood up and took a few casual steps to the left, casually taking my phone from my pocket as I did so. I flipped the phone to camera mode and held it up, pretending to be dialling a number. Holding the phone as steady as I could, I zoomed in on Morag's laptop and took a quick close-up of the screen. Then I casually went back to sitting casually and looking casual.

While the rehearsal on the stage carried on, I looked at the picture I'd taken. Luckily, I'd caught the laptop just right and, with only a few minor adjustments to the image, the open email was readable. Unluckily, only the email's header and the last section of text had been visible on screen – Morag must have scrolled down the email before leaving it.

What I could see was this:

**To:** customer.services@zippyprinters.co.uk
**From:** morag.wellington_barnes@ultranet.net
**Subject:** Posters advertising The Poisoned Arrow

because when the first batch of posters were delivered six weeks ago they were printed back to front. I phoned you. I was not happy.

The second batch was delivered five weeks ago. They proudly announced a performance of The Poisoned Marrow starring Sir Golbert Smidge. I phoned you again. I was not happy. I told you that if these posters weren't correctly printed and delivered to me within two days their would be trouble.

Two days later, no posters. I phoned you. I was not happy. I cancelled the entire order. I went to another print shop, who got them done the same day. And for less money.

So, no, I will not be paying this bill you've sent me. You can take it and stick it in your poisoned marrow.

Yours sincerely
Morag Wellington-Barnes

At first, this snapshot didn't appear to tell me anything useful; Morag was simply having a moan at someone who'd mucked up a printing job.

However, as I glanced through it a second time, I saw something which confirmed one of Tom's suspicions. There was evidence here that it *was* Morag who had dropped those pieces of paper. Or, at least, that it was Morag who had drawn that plan of the theatre, showing the entrances and exits.

Can you see it too?

Halfway down that email's text, Morag had written 'their would be trouble', when she should have put 'there would be trouble'. Exactly the same mistake that appeared on the plan of the theatre.

Meanwhile, the rehearsal was continuing. From what I'd seen so far, the play looked like it might turn out to be pretty good. Once they'd stopped arguing about the big battle scene, anyway.

When the session finished, I had a sudden shock when I thought I'd have to endure Tom's yattering all the way home. Then I remembered that, from there, our houses were in opposite directions and I felt OK again.

As I headed for the bus stop, I was already jotting some thoughts down in my notebook (see opposite). Daylight was rapidly fading. I glanced back and in the large field behind the theatre I could see two or three horses. They were cantering around and flicking their manes.

*I wonder what they'd make of the pantomime horses those actors were on about*, I thought. I smiled to myself and went back to my notebook.

# A Page From My Notebook

**On the plus side:** I've made a couple of important discoveries.

**On the minus side:** Those discoveries point in completely OPPOSITE directions.

**Events at the rehearsal suggest:** Sir Gilbert may have a MOTIVE for planning a crime, but Morag is the one who is most implicated in putting such a plan together (she drew that plan of the theatre).

Could they BOTH be involved? If so, WHY? If not, then one or other of my so-called important discoveries is almost certainly wrong.

# CHAPTER
## Five

*GET HERE. NOW.*

Izzy's texting was often straightforward and to the point, but the three-word message she sent me just as I arrived home was even more concise than usual.

I texted back: *See you at school? Just got home.*

She replied: *Have solved case.*

Twenty minutes later, I was standing in her glittery, fluffy, spangly, multi-coloured, multi-beanbag room. I was also out of breath because I'd run the last hundred metres or so.

'You are so unfit, Saxby,' she tutted, swivelling around on the chair beside her computer.

'The case,' I wheezed. 'What have you found?'

'Honestly,' she said, collecting up a handful of

printouts, 'if you don't start getting more exercise you're going to start storing up problems for when you're older.'

'The *case*?' I gasped.

'Yes,' she said. 'Good thing I decided to help out on this one. That list of names you gave me has sorted out the whole thing. After I'd done some initial research, I had an idea and showed the list to my mum. It turns out that she already knows who most of these people are and had lots of useful information.' (Izzy's mum was a sharply-suited executive, the sort of business woman who has two secretaries and a really smart briefcase.)

'OK, whatcha got?' I asked.

Izzy turned the list so that I could see the names. 'Seventeen of these people are likely to be, by most estimates, the seventeen wealthiest people in this area. You've got the owners of six large companies in the middle of town, the regional directors of another four international companies, one retired professional footballer, two guys who create office software, a property developer, the man who invented the self-fastening shoelace and two old ladies who just happen to have a heck of a lot of money.'

'Wow,' I said. 'You never know who lives just around the corner, do you?'

'You'd be surprised,' said Izzy. 'By far the richest person is the property developer. This name here – Jason Dreasdale. He buys land and old buildings, puts up new buildings and sells them on. It's thought his fortune runs into several million pounds.'

'Wow,' I said again. 'He could fund saving the Turtle-Shell all by himself.' Something vague stirred at the back of my memory, but I brushed it aside because I wanted to find out what else Izzy had discovered.

'What about the other five names on the list?' I asked. 'The ones marked with asterisks?'

'They are, going from top to bottom,' said Izzy, pointing a finger down the list, 'the mayor, the leader of the town council, a member of parliament, another member of parliament who happens to be in charge of town councils and the council's head of planning.'

'What does a head of planning do?' I asked.

'He authorises who gets to build what and where all over town,' said Izzy.

'You've done a great job, Izzy, as always,' I said, 'but, umm, I don't quite see how this information solves the case.'

Izzy handed me back the list. 'It's very simple,' she said. 'There *is* no case.'

'Huh?'

'All those doubts you had about Tom's suspicions?

You were right first time. There's nothing going on, no robbery being planned, nothing. You and Tom are reading far too much into far too little.'

'What makes you say that?'

'A couple of Christmases ago, my mum organised a big charity event for her office. Similar kind of thing, but a posh dinner and ballroom dancing rather than a play. And guess what? She wrote down a list almost identical to this one. Well, as far as these first seventeen go, anyway. Why? To make sure that all the most minted guests donated the most money. She even pinpointed them on her seating plan, so her helpers would know where to rattle their collection tins! If the director of this play . . . whatsername?'

'Morag Wellington-Barnes,' I said.

'If she's compiled this list,' said Izzy, 'it will be to give to Sir Gilbert Smudge, so that he knows who he mustn't miss when he's out there gathering donations. Saxby, this is all entirely innocent. Morag has every reason to have a list like this in her pocket.'

'You really think so?' I said quietly.

'Absolutely,' said Izzy. 'You and Tom are barking up the wrong tree.'

A thought occurred to me. 'Wait! What about that plan Morag drew? The one showing the entrances and exits to the theatre?'

'When my mum organised her charity event,' continued Izzy, 'she drew a plan exactly the same. Not of the Rackham Road theatre, of course – a plan of the hotel where they were going to hold the event.'

'Eh? Why?'

'You wouldn't believe the forms that have to be filled in if you want to hold a public event,' Izzy replied. 'The Turtle-Shell is like any other venue – it has to have a licence to put on shows. Several of the official forms that have to be sent in are about Health and Safety regulations. Morag will have had to show the authorities that the theatre has proper fire exits, access for emergency vehicles and all that. I bet you didn't know about any of that, did you?'

'Er, no,' I admitted.

'Actually, neither did I, not until Mum mentioned it. But once again it shows that Morag isn't planning a robbery of any kind, in any way, at any time.'

I had to admit what Izzy was saying made sense. I folded the list up again and put it in my pocket.

'Now then,' said Izzy, 'if you'll excuse me, I've really got to get that science homework done. And so have you.'

As I walked home, I felt more confused than a hedgehog in a hairbrush factory. I also felt very relieved. It seemed that, just for once, my worst fears wouldn't come true.

Even so, I couldn't help also feeling a certain . . . hmm, I'm not sure what you'd call it. Worry? Nervousness? Something small and elusive was still nagging away in the back of my mind.

So, had I simply misinterpreted Morag Wellington-Barnes's apparently strange decisions (the keeping on of the house lights, the ditching of the play's minor characters, etc)? Was it all merely a question of her doing things her way?

Technically, I still had a motive for Sir Gilbert to plan a robbery. However, once I took everything else that might raise suspicion out of the picture (the plan, the list, the odd decisions), it left me with absolutely no reason to suspect Sir Gilbert at all. Or anyone else, for that matter.

But even so . . .

I couldn't help thinking about those other five names, the ones marked with an asterisk. I could see why those people might be on the overall guest list, but why were they on this *special* list, this list which otherwise only included those seventeen names? If Morag had compiled that list for Sir Gilbert's benefit, as Izzy had suggested, then why had she added these other five? And why mark them separately?

In the end, I had to tell myself to stop letting this whole business prey on my mind! There was no evidence that anything sinister was going on. None at all. I could relax. I could let it go. I could move on to other things. Hey, I could even get my science homework done!

Little did I know . . .

# CHAPTER
# Six

THE FOLLOWING DAY, AT SCHOOL, I explained Izzy's findings to Tom. I didn't mention the lingering doubts that were still hanging around in my head, like sullen teenagers on a street corner.

'Hmmm, I dunno,' said Tom. 'I still have lingering doubts.'

'Well, I haven't,' I lied. 'I think we can safely say that this is a case I can label *The Adventure of the No Case After All.*'

'Oh well,' sighed Tom. 'At least it gives me a chance to concentrate on the play. I've got some radical and very exciting ideas for the battle scene. I'm sure Morag will stick her nose up at them, still, I can but try.'

At that, he swanned off to geography. Tom had given

me a ticket to Friday's performance (each member of the cast was allocated a few freebies), and by the time Friday arrived I was really looking forward to it.

I arrived at the Turtle-Shell in plenty of time so that I could pop backstage and wish Tom and everyone else good luck.

'Agh!' squealed Tom, already in his medieval peasant costume and plastered in stage make-up. 'You can't say that! It's bad luck! We actors are very superstitious! You mustn't say the G-L phrase. You must say "Break a leg".'

'Really? I'm supposed to wish you'd break a leg?' I asked.

'Yes,' said Tom. 'Quickly!'

'OK. Break a leg.'

'Thanks. Much appreciated. By the way, Morag actually *liked* my radical and very exciting ideas for the battle scene. Everyone's going to love it.'

I gave him a quick thumbs-up and went back to the main auditorium. The performance was due to begin in a few minutes.

It turned out that my seat was next to Tom's parents. I'd met them before, during the case of *The Stranger in the Mirror*.

'Hello Saxby,' they said with a cheery nod.

Tom's mum was a slight, plainly-dressed woman. If Tom hadn't told me, I'd never have guessed that she could speak fluent Mandarin and was a fully qualified plumber.

Tom's dad was a chunky man with a moustache that couldn't make up its mind which direction to grow in. He worked for the local council, in charge of the drains. There was a faint whiff of wet earth about him.

'I expect there's quite a few people here tonight you know from work,' I said to him. 'The guest list includes several council officials.'

'Yes,' said Tom's dad. 'I've been seeing faces I know since I got here. One or two surprises, too, I must say.'

'Surprises?' I said. 'Why's that?'

Tom's dad nodded in the direction of a weasly little man sitting a couple of rows in front of us. 'That's our head of planning. He wouldn't normally get invited to a staff party, let alone a charity do. He's a miserable little skunk.'

Head of planning? Ah, yes, one of the asterisked names Izzy had told me about back in Chapter Five.

'Hmm,' I pondered. 'Who's the other surprise you mentioned?'

'Oh, Jason Dreasdale,' said Tom's dad, pointing over his shoulder at chest level so it couldn't be seen from behind. 'The only person I know who's even more poisonous than our head of planning.'

Dreasdale, the property developer, was sitting beside

one of the aisles, several rows behind me. He reminded me of a bulldog: he was broad and bald, with an enormous mouth and limbs which looked like they were designed for levering tree trunks out of the ground. His nose looked like it had lost a fight with a lawnmower, and down his right cheek – from eye to chin – was a creased and livid scar.

He was so wide, he kept elbowing the woman sitting next to him in the ribs. He was ignoring her protests. The look on his face was a mixture of impatience, simmering temper and more impatience.

My stomach suddenly felt as if it was dropping towards the centre of the earth.

*Of course!* Why hadn't I realised before?

I knew more about Jason Dreasdale than Izzy had told me. I knew there was a direct link between Jason Dreasdale and Tom's first suspicions about Morag!

Have you spotted it?

That scar. That nose. It was *Dreasdale* who Tom had seen talking to Morag in the theatre car park! Dreasdale was the mysterious man Tom had called an 'obvious villain'. So . . .

Was Izzy wrong about there being no case?

Was something going on here after all?

Quickly, I turned back to Tom's dad. 'Why is it surprising to see Jason Dreasdale here? Has he got some connection with this place?'

'Connection?' said Tom's dad. 'No, not at all, not unless you count the Dreasdale Tower.'

'The Dreasdale Tower?'

'The huge block of flats he wants to build on this site. It's Jason Dreasdale who wants to bulldoze this theatre.'

'*W-W-What?*' I spluttered.

'Oh yeah, he's been trying to buy it for years, but the theatre people have always just about scraped together the rent in time, so the council have never allowed him to get his greedy mitts on it. There's no love lost between the council and Jason Dreasdale, that's for sure. That's why I'm surprised to see him here. He's not exactly a fan of this place. Oh well, I guess whoever invited the likes of Dreasdale and our head of planning had their reasons.'

Ideas were beginning to stir in the dusty storage cupboard tucked away under the stairs at the back of my brain. Tom's dad leaned closer to me to whisper. I think that smell of wet soil was coming from his coat.

'Between you and me, Saxby,' he muttered, 'I've heard some nasty things about Jason Dreasdale. It's said that he's resorted to all kinds of dirty tricks to make his millions. Sabotaged rivals, threatened people, all sorts of ugly stuff. I'm surprised you've never come across him before, you being a detective. Anyway, I'm glad tonight's fund-raiser looks like it'll go well. It'd be a crime to bulldoze this place.'

At that moment, a fanfare sounded. The stage curtains slowly parted and the play began. Tom (as Wilbert the peasant boy) and half a dozen others were in the middle of a banquet. Tom had the first line.

''Tis evil work afoot, my lords, when the Baron doth plot to seize the throne from our noble King Lionel!'

The first half of the performance went very well. However, my attention wandered. The things Tom's dad had said kept returning to my thoughts, like echoes in a cave.

. . . *Whoever invited the likes of Dreasdale and our head of planning had their reasons* . . .

. . . *It'd be a crime to bulldoze this place* . . .

Suddenly, it was the interval. After a round of applause had died down, there was another round of applause as Sir Gilbert Smudge appeared from behind the curtains.

'Ladies and gentlemen,' he declared in his fruity tones, 'it's time for the most important part of the evening. Apart from the after-show drinks at the pub, that is!'

Laughter all round. While Sir Gilbert told us about the wonderful history of the Turtle-Shell and its importance as a community theatre, I twisted around in my seat to take another look at Jason Dreasdale.

He was texting someone, half his attention on his phone and half on Sir Gilbert.

And at that moment, the truth finally dawned on me.

Tom's suspicions about Morag had been correct. But he – and I – had failed to see the full picture.

I leaped to my feet. Pulling my phone from my pocket, I ran for the main entrance of the theatre, passing Dreasdale on the way. I had to raise the alarm, and quickly. And I had to do it without causing a panic in the auditorium.

First, I thought to myself, call Izzy and get her to alert the police. Second, go backstage and alert Tom and the rest of the cast (revealing to Morag that the game was up, if needs be!).

The whole horrible scenario was now clear to me. It worked like this:

1. Dreasdale wants the theatre flattened.

2. *But!* The theatre is about to stage a major fund-raiser that will keep it safe.

3. *So!* He resorts to underhand tactics. He decides to ruin the theatre's efforts by *robbing* the fund-raiser! The point of this robbery is not so much to get loads of money, but to stop that cash benefiting the theatre!

4. He wants help from inside the theatre, so he recruits Morag into his scheme. Morag – in exchange for a large amount of money, presumably – can organise the performance to make a raid on it easier (those odd decisions of hers, remember), *and* place Dreasdale and various influential councillors and politicians on the guest list.

5. *Then!* On the night of the performance, a gang of armed thugs raids the theatre sometime after the interval, when Sir Gilbert has collected up all the charity donations.

6. *Result?* The Turtle-Shell goes bust. Dreasdale can move in! (As a bonus, those influential councillors and politicians having been through this traumatic robbery themselves are left with the impression that the place is a crime-ridden menace and probably won't object to Dreasdale's bulldozing it! *And*, as another bonus, Dreasdale has the proceeds from the robbery to use when buying the theatre!)

I hurtled out of the theatre. It was dark. A thick fog had descended and there was nobody in sight. With trembling fingers, I dialled Izzy's number.

'Are you sure about this?' gasped Izzy. 'Isn't Dreasdale taking a big risk?'

'Dreasdale stands to make a fortune from all the flats he'll build,' I said. 'It's well worthwhile for him!'

'But why has he put himself at the scene of the crime?' cried Izzy. 'If he'd never normally go to the Turtle-Shell, why has he got himself added to the guest list?'

'Perfect alibi,' I said. 'He gets himself robbed with everyone else and it diverts suspicion away from him. Who's going to suspect a robbery victim of staging the robbery?'

'But if the plan works, he wouldn't *need* an alibi,' protested Izzy, 'because he wouldn't be suspected in the first place. Why should the plan require Dreasdale to be sitting there in the audience?'

I thought back to what I'd seen at the end of the play's first half, and to that six-point scenario. Suddenly, my stomach felt like it had gone right through the centre of the earth and come out again the other side.

I could see why Dreasdale would need to be in the audience. I knew who he must have been texting!

Do you?

'Uh-oh,' I said, my voice wobbling slightly. 'He needs someone in the audience to signal a Go to the gang, someone he trusts completely. Himself! He's just texted the gang that it's time to move in!'

'I'll call the police right now,' said Izzy.

'Call me back as soon as you've contacted them. I'll go backstage, so when you ring me I can tell them the cops are on their way.'

I snapped my phone shut and hurried back inside.

In the auditorium, Sir Gilbert was collecting up the last of the charity contributions. A short line of audience members – including the mayor and Jason Dreasdale – were standing at the front being applauded while Morag was poised with a marker pen on the stage, writing down the running total of contributions on a flip chart.

I skirted the audience, hurrying down one side of the auditorium, along the line of elongated, window-covering curtains. *Stay calm*, I told myself, *don't rush, don't raise the alarm too early, don't let Dreasdale or Morag know they've been rumbled. Go backstage, talk to Tom, and then when Izzy calls —*

I stopped dead.

My phone had gone.

I must have dropped it outside! It must be lying somewhere on the forecourt gravel!

Luckily, my loud yelp of horror was swamped by the

audience's clapping. Sir Gilbert acknowledged the crowd with a teary smile of gratitude.

'My friends,' he boomed, 'our theatre is safe once more, thanks to your wonderful generosity. And now, we shall commence the second half of our play, and we have something very —'

His voice was cut off as the heavy door clunked shut behind me. I took a few steps across the gravel, my footsteps crunching loudly.

And now we're back where we began, at the start of Chapter One.

It was 8.45 p.m. The fog was thickening.

Where was that blasted phone? I bent down and scooped it up. Good – I hadn't missed Izzy's call. I pocketed my phone and stood.

And then I heard them: the footsteps. My heart began to thump.

Suddenly, out of the darkness, emerging through the mist came those six hulking figures – tall, heavy, smothered in dark coats, each wearing a horrible Halloween pumpkin mask. I was terrified. One crunching step and they'd know I was there.

At that moment, my phone trilled. Loudly.

The man in front stopped. 'Is someone there?' he boomed. 'Show yourself! Now!'

He twitched an arm to usher the others forward.

I didn't dare breathe. The only thought going through my head was: *Why do I let myself get into these messes?*

In an instant, I'd switched my phone off.

The pumpkin-heads were only a few metres away from me.

By my left shoulder was that hideous statue I told you about, the one which stands on the forecourt and shows four human figures striking dramatic poses.

It was my only hope. One big step took me into the middle of those four figures. I crouched slowly, carefully, silently. My heart was tearing and my head felt as if it was about to burst.

Was the statue enough to conceal me? Was the foggy darkness enough to hide me from view?

'C'mon, let's get inside,' grunted the one in front, the one carrying the big canvas bag. 'We're on a timetable here. Remember, he wants it done fast, he wants noise, he wants a few bones broken.'

He opened the canvas bag. Baseball bats were handed out. 'Right, let's go!'

Two of them headed for the emergency exit on the left side of the building, two for the one on the right, and the last two barged through the main doors behind me.

I was too late! It was happening right now!

That terrifying gang of thieves were entering the crowded theatre and there was nothing I could do about it.

# CHAPTER
# Seven

I FELT TOTALLY HELPLESS.

The only thing that was racing through my brain was: *Whaddoidonow? Whaddoidonow? Ohnowhaddoidonow?*

I followed the last two pumpkin-heads and returned to the main entrance to the theatre. Cautiously, I pressed my nose to one of the door's glass panels and peered inside.

I was just in time to see them raise their baseball bats high above their heads and run into the brightly lit auditorium. They yelled a murderous, blood-curdling war cry as they bounded forward. I could see the other pumpkin-heads charging in from either side at the same time.

They all came screaming out into an auditorium that was . . .

Empty.

'Huh?' I cried. I poked a finger behind my glasses, rubbed my eyes and looked again.

The auditorium was empty. No audience. Every last seat audience-free. Gone. Vanished. *L'audience ce n'est pas la.*

'What in the name of Sherlock Holmes is going on?' I gasped to myself.

For a moment or two, all six pumpkin-heads were equally startled and confused. They stood there, bats raised, pumpkin masks turning this way and that, standing in the middle of rows and rows of vacant seats.

Suddenly, a dozen or more figures stepped out from where they'd been hiding behind the curtained sides of the auditorium. Several of them were armed.

'Police! Drop your weapons! Down on the floor!'

The pumpkin-heads were so bewildered they all did exactly as they were told. I was so bewildered I almost did the same myself.

The plain-clothes police officers quickly descended on the pumpkin-heads, pinning them to the ground. Then, from behind the closed curtains on the stage, another plain-clothes officer led out Jason Dreasdale, his wrists snapped into handcuffs. (This officer was the woman I'd seen sitting next to him, the one he'd kept elbowing! She must have nabbed him only seconds after I'd gone to look for my phone!)

Behind them came Morag. At first, I thought she was under arrest too. But one of the officers ran over to her and put a hand on her shoulder. I could tell he was asking her if she was OK, and she nodded that she was. He gave her a gentle pat on the back.

Dreasdale, seething with rage, spun around and yelled at Morag. Nothing of what he said is repeatable here. Three officers pounced on him and dragged him away.

By now, I'd come to my senses. Well, a bit, anyway. Remembering that plan Morag had drawn and what I already knew about where the theatre stood, I could work out where the entire audience must have gone.

Can you?

Morag's drawing showed double doors at the rear of the backstage area, opening out on to the neighbouring field. Everyone must have got up out of their seats and trooped over the stage and out of the back of the building.

I hurried around the side of the Turtle-Shell. I took out my phone as I jogged along and switched it back on. There was a text from Izzy: *The police already know!!??!!*

'No kidding,' I muttered to myself.

The sight that greeted me when I got to the field behind the theatre was nothing short of amazing. The entire audience was standing in a huge ring around the perimeter of the field. Coloured spotlights had been rigged up and glowed eerily in the swirling fog. Across the centre of the field, the big battle scene of *The Poisoned Arrow* was being played out, complete with real horses. *Real* horses.

Sir Gilbert Smudge did a spectacular job of acting King Lionel's death. There was just enough blood to make it look nicely yukky. Tom was very good when it came to wielding his sword and fighting the evil Baron Thornicroft.

The overall effect was wonderful. Characters (and horses) kept moving in and out of the rolling mist that enshrouded the whole field. The spotlights gave everything an air of creepy mystery.

And the crowd loved every minute of it. Clearly, nobody had the slightest clue that something even more dramatic was happening back inside the building.

*If only you knew*, I thought to myself. *If only all of you knew!*

I stood and watched the rest of the performance. It was chilly out there, but nobody minded. (However, I made sure I kept back from the horses, in case they set off my animal hair allergy, but I was fine.)

The play ended with a mighty cry from Tom: 'Our dead king be avenged! Knowest thou that justice be upheld! To glory!' There was so much clapping and cheering I thought it would never end. The cast took their bows from the middle of the muddy patch that the battle had stirred up. Sir Gilbert got the biggest cheer of all.

The audience gradually dispersed, amid mutterings of 'Best play I've seen in years', and 'Clever idea, that', and 'Oh dear, I think I've stood in horse poo.' The cast regrouped in the backstage area of the theatre. I trotted over to where Tom was busy scraping some of the mud-splats off his costume.

'I told you I had radical and very exciting ideas for the battle scene,' he declared. 'And they worked brilliantly.'

'Yes.' I smiled. 'Yes, they did. But what if it had been tipping down with rain?'

'We'd have got wet! You can't let the weather spoil great art! Although,' he added, 'I still don't know why Morag said yes to my ideas.'

'Oh, I think I might now have the answer to that one,' I said. 'Excuse me, I must go and have a chat with Morag.'

I found her sitting with her legs dangling over the edge of the stage. The auditorium was now deserted. You'd never have guessed what had happened. I sat down beside her and quietly let her know what I'd seen.

'Tom told me you're a great detective,' she said. 'So I assume you've worked out what's been going on?'

'I have,' I said. 'At long last. How much did Dreasdale offer you, to co-operate with his plan?'

'Oh, a lot,' said Morag, rolling her eyes slightly. 'A lot. And for a little while, I have to admit I was tempted. I really was.'

'What changed your mind?'

'You know, I think it was the play,' said Morag. '*The Poisoned Arrow* is all about doing the right thing and making sure the bad guys don't have their way. It reminded me that I had a duty not to let Dreasdale get away with it, no matter what. Besides, this building is important to a lot of people. Some things are far more valuable than money.'

'So you pretended to go along with Dreasdale's plan?'

'Yes. I went to the police a couple of weeks ago. They've been after Dreasdale for a while, but they've never had enough evidence to make a serious charge stick. They needed to catch him red-handed, so they came up with the idea of tonight's ambush. Now they've got the whole gang, and they've got his phone, along with the text he sent telling them to attack the building.'

'I'm really sorry,' I said. 'All this week I've completely misinterpreted your actions.'

'How?' she said.

'Well, for a start,' I said, 'you reduced the number of people in the cast. The *real* reason you did that was because you knew those pumpkin-heads would go backstage and flush out anyone there before they could escape through the back doors. You were trying to keep as many people as possible out of harm's way, just in case.

'And you kept all the house lights on during the performance. The *real* reason you did that was to make sure that the pumpkin-heads would be seen the instant they turned up, giving the audience the best possible chance of keeping away from them.

'And you seated the special guests all over the auditorium. The *real* reason you did that was to make it as hard as possible for the pumpkin-heads to get to them. They'd have to run all over the place to reach all their targets.'

She grinned at me. 'Correct, correct and correct. But then Tom came up with the brilliant idea of having the big battle scene in the field outside.'

'Right,' I said. 'He didn't know it but his idea fitted in

71

perfectly with the police ambush. It got the entire audience out of the way at just the right time. He's still amazed you said yes.'

'Well, let's let him think it was down to his magnetic personality,' said Morag. 'I'm relieved it wasn't tipping down with rain, or we'd have had to abandon the idea. The quieter we can keep the ambush, the better. I don't want anything to upset what's been an unexpectedly successful evening.'

'Maybe you could have pretended that the ambush was part of the play?' I said brightly. Morag stared at me wearily. 'Or, maybe not, rubbish idea,' I muttered.

Only one difficulty remained. Dreasdale was rich and powerful and he now knew that Morag had led him into a trap. What if he sent someone after her, for revenge?

'The police did warn me about that,' said Morag when I mentioned it to her. 'But they're helping me take care of it. There's no way I'm going to be bullied by the likes of Jason Dreasdale. He doesn't scare me.'

'Good for you,' I said. 'But if you ever need help, Tom knows where to find me. Talking of Tom, I'm going to see if I can cadge a lift home off his parents. See ya!'

I arrived back home mulling over what a strange and eventful evening it had been. I hurried out to my shed, determined to get some notes down on paper while the whole thing was still fresh in my mind.

It was only then that I remembered something Izzy had said. I looked at my watch. 9.38 p.m. I still hadn't done my science homework. Hmmm.

Everyone agreed that the play had been a triumph, and Tom got all the credit for the battle-in-the-field idea. He boasted about it for days. No, weeks. No, come to think of it, he was still boring the whole school with it for the rest of that term. Some things never change.

Sir Gilbert Smudge got rave reviews for his performance in *The Poisoned Arrow*. The following week he was offered a leading role on Broadway in New York. He was back on the A-list. He insisted on having Morag hired as director.

And as for Jason Dreasdale, well he, plus his gang, plus half a dozen crooked accountants and lawyers he employed, all got prison sentences a few months later. The police had a field day unravelling the web of corruption and shady deals that spread through his entire organisation. I had a good laugh every time the media revealed another major crime he was being charged with.

Case closed.

# THE NIGHTMARE
## OF
# ROOM 9B

# CHAPTER ONE

IF YOU HAPPEN TO TURN up at St Egbert's School one lunchtime, and it happens to be a day when I'm not in the middle of an investigation, ask me to tell you all about the Three Most Important Elements of Crime Detection. I can't really go into details now, otherwise I'll use up the rest of this book. I'll simply say that these Important Elements are: 1) Motive, 2) Method, and 3) Opportunity. In other words: *why* they did it, *how* they did it and *when* they did it.

I'm sure you've heard me mention these things plenty of times before. The point is, when you've investigated as many strange and mysterious happenings as I have, you start to take things like this for granted.

And you shouldn't.

Mind you, not everyone would agree with me about these Important Elements in the first place. I recently read a huge book about street crime in big cities and the cops in that book definitely rate the Important Elements as: 1) Evidence (weapons, DNA, etc), 2) Witnesses (anyone who saw it happen, or saw the bad guy running away), and 3) Confessions (getting the bad guy to own up). Mostly, they don't need to worry about a crime's motive.

But they're tough cops, doing a tough job in tough places. I'm not. They have loads of people and special laboratories at their disposal. I don't. They are the Law, they have authority on their side. I'm a schoolboy, for goodness' sake! Detectives like me have to rely on brainpower alone.

Anyway, sorry, I seem to be drifting off the point here . . .

What I'm saying is, never make assumptions about these Important Elements. Motive especially. Because sometimes, just sometimes, they can turn out to be really *weird*.

Detectives have to be rational. Logical. Detached from the situation. 'Dispassionate' is another word my thesaurus suggests. You mustn't let personal feelings interfere with your thinking. Do you ever see great fictional detectives like Hercule Poirot or Philip Marlowe running off in tears because things are getting a bit much? No, you bloomin' well don't!

And it's this need for logic and being dispassionate that can make the occasional weirdness in the Important Elements very hard to untangle.

Here's a perfect example of how motive-madness can throw a spanner in the works: a case I've called *The Nightmare of Room 9B*.

It started on one of those very rare mornings when the weather is in the Goldilocks zone – not too hot, not too cold. Just right.

Even better, it was a school day but the whole of St Egbert's was closed! There had been an accident involving the electricity supply and a jug of school gravy. St Egbert's wouldn't be open again for the rest of the week. The Head was furious. The rest of us were delighted. I was double-delighted because I still hadn't done my science homework and now I had a few extra days to get it finished.

I was in my Crime HQ, flopped into my battered old leather armchair – my Thinking Chair – and I was weighing up two alternatives. Should I do my science homework or sort through some of the case notes in my filing cabinet? Hmmm . . .

I'd just got a pile of case notes out on my desk when

there was a tap at the shed door. 'Come in!' I cried.

It was Mrs Hardyman, one of our school dinner ladies. I'd always thought of her as slightly scary. She reminded me of something plastic left in a hot oven: everything about her seemed melty and elongated. Even at the best of times her face was thin-lipped and sour, but now it appeared to have been soaked in vinegar for a couple of days. She stepped into the shed as if walking on broken glass.

'Hello,' I said, as cheerfully as I could. 'How can I help you?'

'H'lo Saxby,' she said in a quiet, doleful voice. 'I asked a couple of teachers and they said you might be able to help me.'

'I'll do my best,' I said, smiling. I offered her my Thinking Chair and I made a space for myself amongst the case files on the desk.

Her eyes flickered around the shed, taking in the piles of gardening and DIY stuff I'm forced to share my Crime HQ with. 'I've only come here because the police don't want to know and I can't afford a proper detective.'

'Er, OK,' I said, still smiling.

'I wouldn't normally ask some kid I hardly know for help,' she said. 'Especially one of that St Egbert's mob.'

'Er, OK,' I said, still smiling.

'I'm scraping the bottom of the barrel here. I've come

to the end of my tether.' Tears began to well up in her eyes. Suddenly, I felt very sorry for her.

I don't like it when people start crying in my shed. I guess it's something to do with that stay-logical-and-detached business I mentioned.

Quickly, I tugged the hanky from my pocket and handed it to her, hoping she wouldn't notice the bits I'd already sneezed on. She dabbed at her eyes and handed it back. As she glanced at me, there was genuine sorrow on her face and I felt sorry for her all over again. She sniffed and straightened herself up.

'Thank you,' she said. 'Sorry, I've hardly slept the last couple of nights. I've been so worried.'

'What about?' I asked. 'What's the problem?'

'It's my boy, Nat,' she said. 'He's a student over at the university. He's been home for the past couple of days and he's hardly left his room. He won't eat and he just sits there looking unhappy.'

'Why?'

'He was arrested by the police on Tuesday. They've let him out on bail, but they're charging him with theft. The university have suspended him and he'll be expelled if he's found guilty. They're saying he stole a laptop computer from his tutor, Dr Shroeder.'

'And, umm . . . did he?'

'Of course not,' cried Mrs Hardyman. 'He's never

been in trouble in his life. He's a good boy. Someone has set him up! He's innocent!'

'And who's accusing him of this theft?' I asked.

'He's accusing himself,' said Mrs Hardyman. 'And his three best friends are backing him up.'

# CHAPTER TWO

I FROWNED SLIGHTLY, AND MY mouth squidged into the shape of a comma. 'Soooo,' I said, 'your son Nat has *admitted* that he stole a computer.'

'Yes,' said Mrs Hardyman, 'but he didn't do it.'

I paused. I was trying to think of exactly the right way to express what I was thinking.

'A computer has been stolen,' I said, slowly, 'and Nat says he stole it. And, you say, his three best friends also say he stole it.'

'Yes,' replied Mrs Hardyman.

'But he didn't really steal it?'

'No.'

'How do you know that?'

'Because he's a good boy,' said Mrs Hardyman. 'He

wouldn't do such a thing. He's never been in trouble in his life.'

'So why would he and his friends lie about something like that?' I asked. 'It's a pretty serious thing to admit to if you didn't do it, isn't it?'

'Someone's forced him to take the blame,' said Mrs Hardyman. 'Someone's bullying him or blackmailing him or something like that. He's a good boy.'

I took a deep breath. 'Umm, Mrs Hardyman, I, er, don't want to appear, umm . . . unkind . . . but, if Nat and three other people all say he's guilty, isn't it just possible that he's, er, guilty?'

'Then where is this stolen computer?' Mrs Hardyman pointed out. 'He's said to the police that he's hidden it. What's the point of that? Steal a computer, then hide it so nobody can use it, then own up to stealing it in the first place? It's crackers!'

I had to admit, when you looked at it that way, it did seem odd. 'Tell me all the details,' I said. 'Let's get a clear picture of what's happened.'

'My Nat is twenty years old,' said Mrs Hardyman. 'He's been studying advanced maths at the university for over a year. And he's been doing very well at it, too. He's top of his class. Dr Shroeder says his demonstrations of equation-solving in class are the best he's ever seen.'

'And does he have a lot of friends at uni?' I asked.

'Well, no, just the three, really. He's shy and sensitive, very dedicated to his studies. He's not one of these students you see on telly going to parties all the time and making a lot of noise at three in the morning. He lives at home with me, he eats sensibly and he does his share of the chores.'

'And does he use computers much?' I said. 'I suppose he must do if he's studying maths.'

'Yes, he's got two of them,' said Mrs Hardyman. 'A laptop he's had for years, which he takes to classes with him every day, and a large one on the desk in his room which he bought with money from his part-time job. He works in SuperSave at the weekends. I'm telling you, he'd have no need to steal another one!'

'So what exactly happened?' I said. 'You said he was arrested on Tuesday?'

'Yes,' said Mrs Hardyman. 'The computer was stolen on Monday morning. Dr Shroeder had his laptop in his study at the university. He went for a wee and when he came back the laptop was gone. He was only out of the room for a couple of minutes.'

'And then what happened?'

'When it was clear that the laptop had been stolen, Dr Shroeder went to the head of department's office to report the theft, and they called the police. A couple of officers were asking questions around the campus most of the day. A number of students had seen Nat but none had seen the computer. They dusted for fingerprints in Dr Shroeder's office, but didn't find anything useful. It got to about four o'clock and they hadn't come up with any clues. They were about to go back to the police station when Dr Shroeder came over to them and told them that Nat had just confessed to the theft. And then they took him in for questioning.'

I jotted down a couple of lines in my notebook. 'Was there anything special about this stolen computer?' I asked. 'Was there any particular reason why someone would want to steal it?'

'It was almost brand new, apparently,' said Mrs Hardyman. 'One of those flashy white and silver things you see in adverts, very trendy, can't remember what they're called. Very expensive, too.'

'So the police think it was stolen because it's a really smart piece of high-tech gear?'

'No. When they were questioning Nat, he told them he took it because he thought next week's exam questions might be on it.'

'There's an exam next week?' I asked.

'Yes, an extremely important one. All the maths students are taking it. This exam counts as a quarter of the total marks for their final qualification. I should think any of them would love to get their hands on those exam questions in advance.'

I'm not exactly Mr Brainbox when it comes to maths, but even I could see that something here didn't add up. I could tell at once that Nat had almost certainly lied to the police. Something Mrs Hardyman had told me pretty much ruled out any idea of Nat wanting to get his hands on that exam.

Have you spotted the oddity in what Nat said?

Nat was top of the class. Someone like him would be *least* likely to want to steal exam questions. If that was what he'd told the police, it was highly unlikely to be the truth. (Unless, of course, he *always* cheated in tests . . .? No, Dr Shroeder said his in-class work was the best he's ever seen – you couldn't cheat at that!)

There was more going on here than I'd first thought. If Nat had owned up to taking that computer, why would he then lie about his reasons for doing it?

'What about these three friends of Nat's?' I said. 'How do they fit into the picture?'

'Matt, Jack and Anil have been his best friends for years.'

'Did they all go to St Egbert's?' I asked.

'Oh no, they went to a nice school that was much less rough. Matt and Jack are doing English literature and Anil is doing engineering. They're also shy and sensitive. I thought they were such good boys until they started lying about Nat!'

'How did that come about?'

'The police let Nat go late on Monday. They said they needed more evidence before they could do anything.'

'Wasn't what he'd said enough?'

Mrs Hardyman shook her head. 'The police won't charge someone based on a confession alone and Nat couldn't produce the computer to prove he'd taken it. I think perhaps they realised he was making it all up. He wouldn't talk about it when he got back. I was just glad to have him home. I thought the whole horrible business might blow over and the university would let him return in a few days, but then the police came to the house and arrested him on Tuesday. Now he's out on bail, waiting to be taken to court.'

'Because his friends backed up his story?' I queried.

'Yes,' said Mrs Hardyman. 'They went to the police on Tuesday morning. All three of them said they'd seen Nat come out of Dr Shroeder's room with the laptop. Jack also said he'd seen Nat an hour later carrying the laptop around campus. Anil said he'd seen Nat at lunchtime using the laptop in the library.'

Wait a minute. Something else didn't add up.

Unless two and two had suddenly started equalling five, there was a strange mismatch here. There was a weird inconsistency between what Nat's friends had told the police and what the police had already discovered for themselves on Monday.

Have you noticed what didn't quite make sense?

On Monday, the police had asked questions around the campus. A number of students had said they'd seen Nat but nobody had seen the computer.

Yet Nat's three friends had apparently seen him *with* the computer? At *three* separate times? On the *same* day? Although *nobody* else had seen the stolen laptop? *Only* Nat's own buddies could link him to the crime?

And why hadn't these friends said anything to the police on Monday? Why wait a day?

'Surely the police spotted the contradiction?' I frowned.

'Maybe they did, maybe they didn't,' sighed Mrs Hardyman sadly. 'All I know is that on Tuesday they had enough evidence to charge him. I think they just wanted a result. Something's got to be done about this situation, and quickly. If Nat's not allowed back to class, he'll miss the exam, he'll fail his course, he'll have ruined his whole future! And he's such a good boy!'

'Never fear,' I said. 'Saxby Smart is on the case.'

# A Page From My Notebook

There are a number of possibilities here:

**POSSIBILITY 1:** Mrs Hardyman is right and Nat is being bullied. She said he's the shy and sensitive type, and this wouldn't be the first time I've come across a tactic like that.

**BUT!:** Why would someone go to all the trouble of making Nat own up to the crime? The real thief would risk Nat calling his bluff and leading the police to him, wouldn't he?

**POSSIBILITY 2:** Mrs Hardyman is wrong and Nat is guilty after all. Once again, this wouldn't be the first time I've come across an unlikely robber.

**BUT!:** Why would Nat ADMIT to the theft? If he'd kept quiet, he may never have been discovered - the police were on the point of leaving. I'd be investigating The Mystery of the Nicked Laptop instead!

There is one giant-sized puzzle lurking underneath these possibilities: WHERE IS THE COMPUTER?

**IF NAT TOOK IT**, and has admitted to taking it, why not give it back? Why tell the police he's hidden it?

**IF NAT DIDN'T TAKE IT**, how can we account for what his friends have told the police?

There are some important questions to consider about the REASON for the theft:

   **Question 1:** Was someone after the exam answers? Or . . .

   **Question 2:** Did someone just want a nice fancy laptop? Or . . .

   **Question 3:** Is there a less obvious motive involved? Could it be, for instance, that the thief is in debt and is planning to sell the computer on the quiet?

My plan of action should include:

   • talking to Nat.

   • talking to Dr Shroeder.

   • talking to those three friends of Nat's.

Ah yes! Those friends . . .

   WHAT is going on with them? WHAT? WHAT? WHAT?

# CHAPTER
# Three

NUMEROUS QUESTIONS SURROUNDING NAT'S THREE friends kept preying on my mind.

What kind of friends would rat on their best pal, anyway? No, I shouldn't say that. That's not fair. Suppose I saw one of my friends stealing something: wouldn't I feel I had to do the right thing and tell the truth about what I'd seen? Even if it was upsetting to think that my friend would get into trouble?

But . . .

Why was there that strange mismatch (as I mentioned near the end of the previous chapter)? Was there something going on here that I hadn't accounted for yet?

Or . . .

Could it be that Nat's friends were making a mistake?

Could it be that what they saw was perfectly innocent? What if, following Nat's declaration of guilt, they had *misinterpreted* what they saw? *That* might account for the mismatch.

But . . .

How can you misinterpret seeing someone with a flashy new computer?

I tried to shoo all such thoughts from my mind as I walked over to Mrs Hardyman's house a little later that day. I told myself that I should concentrate on hearing Nat's side of the story, and that I should keep both my mind and my eyes open for clues.

The Hardymans lived only a few streets away from me. Their house was very like mine – rather plain-looking from the outside, a kind of upturned shoebox-shape lined up along the road with a load of other upturned shoebox-shapes.

'He's still in his room,' whispered Mrs Hardyman. 'He wouldn't touch his lunch and I made his favourite – beetroot and pickle sandwich.'

'I see,' I said, feeling glad she hadn't made lunch for me. Then I remembered that on school days she *did* make lunch for me.

I went up to Nat's room, knocked and went in. It was at the top of the house, overlooking the tiny garden and the backs of the houses in the next street along.

There was an enormous wipe-board fixed to one wall. All over it, mathematical formulae were scribbled in long, weaving lines. You didn't have to be a detective to see this guy would definitely not have the same kind of trouble with long division that I've always had!

The rest of the room was what you might call 'neatly cluttered' – full of stuff, but not a tip. A laptop bag was propped against the wardrobe and the entire under-bed space was crammed with books.

Nat himself was sitting at a desk under the window, flicking through a textbook on an e-reader. He had a carefully combed side parting in his hair and his trousers were slightly too short for his legs. He wore glasses and a plain zip-up cardigan. To be perfectly honest, he looked like a bit of a nerd.

'Hello,' I said brightly. 'I'm Saxby Smart.'

''lo,' he grunted, eyeing me suspiciously. '*You* are Saxby?'

'That's right,' I said.

'You're the detective my mum says she's hired?'

'That's right,' I said.

'Good grief,' he muttered. 'How old are you? Are you even a teenager?'

'Er, no, not yet,' I said. I wasn't quite sure if he thought that was a good thing or a bad thing. Hmm, a bad thing probably, from the look on his face. 'Don't worry,' I chirped up, 'I'm brilliant.'

'If you say so,' he said flatly.

'I need to ask you some questions. I assume you're sticking to your story? You're still claiming you stole that computer?'

'Yup.'

'Any chance of you telling me where it is, then?'

'Nope.'

'Any chance of you giving it back?'

'Nope.'

'You've still got it hidden somewhere, have you?'

'Yup.'

'You're going to have to give it back at some point, you know.'

'I don't want to talk about it.' He went back to his reading.

He was starting to annoy me. Just a teeny tiny little bit.

From the angry embarrassment that was flushing his cheeks and turning his bushy eyebrows into a sharp frown, I got the distinct impression that he didn't *know* where that computer was. Which backed up the idea that he was innocent. (Unless, that was, he'd either already sold the computer or he'd stolen it on someone else's behalf and handed it over to them.)

I shook my head. *Stop it*, I told myself, *I'm going to*

*start thinking in circles if I'm not careful!* I decided to try a different line of enquiry.

'Your friends,' I said. 'Matt, Jack and Anil. I'm very puzzled. Why didn't they say anything to the police on Monday, right after the theft? Why did they wait until Tuesday?'

Nat glanced at me, then back at his textbook, then back at me again. 'They knew what I'd done on Monday. But they're my best friends. They gave me a chance to own up first. Do the right thing.'

'And you did own up,' I said. 'But then you wouldn't hand the computer over. You said you'd hidden it. You're still saying you've hidden it. So the police came to a dead end. And then, let me get this straight, your three friends came forward and told the police what they'd seen. How kind of them. You wouldn't give the police proof that you'd stolen the laptop, so your friends stepped in and made sure the police had three witnesses and therefore enough evidence to charge you. You'd think they *wanted* to make sure you'd be charged.'

Nat suddenly slapped the e-reader down on his desk.

'*Enough!*' he shouted. 'Shut up and get out! I don't want some stupid kid hanging around me!'

For a moment or two I was too shocked to speak. Then I started with, 'But —'

'But nothing! Go on, get out! It's got nothing to do with you! I stole a computer, I'll take the consequences and that's the end of it! *Get out!*'

Without another word, I scuttled quickly out of Nat's room and back down the stairs. Mrs Hardyman had heard the shouts and came hurrying along, apologising for her son's rudeness and assuring me that he was a good boy who'd never been in trouble before in his life. I told her not to worry and that I would now go and carry on my investigation. No matter what Nat thought about it.

I went over to Muddy's house. My great friend George 'Muddy' Whitehouse was St Egbert's School's Number One Mr Fixit, and I needed to borrow one of his gadgets.

I found him working away in the garage attached to the house – or his Development Laboratory, as he prefers people to call it. Whereas Nat's room was what you might call 'neatly cluttered', Muddy's laboratory was what you might call 'disgustingly heaped with every sort of spare part and broken machine you can imagine'.

He was turning dials on a piece of electronic equipment, making a circuit board attached to the wall shoot out flashes and showers of sparks.

'Woohoo!' He beamed. 'Nice one!'

'Isn't that thing appallingly dangerous?' I asked nervously.

Muddy shrugged. 'Well, only if you touch it, or go near it, or you aren't wearing rubber boots. Otherwise, it's fine.' He took off the plastic goggles he was wearing to reveal clearly defined clean patches around his eyes. He looked like a panda in reverse.

We chatted for a while and I told him all about the Hardyman case. 'Do you have a small recording device of some kind that I can borrow?' I asked.

'Ooooh, like, y'know, a wire?' said Muddy gleefully. 'Like undercover cops use in movies?'

'No, like schoolboy detectives use to record ordinary conversations,' I tutted.

'Oh,' said Muddy, disappointed.

'I've already written down heaps of notes,' I said, 'and I've still got several people to talk to. I thought I'd record my chats with them and write up any observations later on.'

Muddy ferreted around in a couple of cardboard boxes, then produced a regular handset with a couple of extra bits sticking out of it. 'I adapted this from my mum's old mobile phone,' he said. 'It records for a couple of hours before it needs a recharge. I was trying to make something that would automatically turn voice messages into written ones, but for some reason they kept coming out in Swahili.'

'Never mind,' I said, 'it's only the recording function I need. Thanks.'

'Is this case turning out to be a real brain-mangler, then?'

I sighed and gave my glasses a quick polish on my sleeve. 'I have to admit,' I said, 'my talk with Nat has only made the entire mystery seem even more alarmingly deep and complex than ever. I think it's looking less and less likely that he *did* commit the crime. I think. But if he *didn't* commit the crime, what sort of terrible hold has the *real* crook got over him? Must be something pretty extreme. And *what* is going on with those friends of his?'

'Maybe they're not friends at all,' said Muddy. 'Maybe they're out to get him for some reason.'

'Hmm, dunno,' I muttered. 'Every angle I look at this problem from, all I can see are more problems. Anyway, thanks for this I'll see you later.'

'Hang on!' cried Muddy. He dived back into his cardboard boxes and came up with a small camera to which he'd attached a big lens. 'I've been itching to try out the new Whitehouse Snoop-o-Zoom Mark 2. I'm coming with you!'

I groaned. 'Do you have to?' I said, one hand over my eyes. 'Do you really, really, really have to?'

'Yes.' He nodded, grinning. 'I want to see if the students at uni are like the students on telly, going to parties all the time and making a lot of noise at three in the morning!'

# CHAPTER
# Four

'AWWW, WOW, LOOK AT THAT! And that! And that! Ooooh!'

'Muddy,' I growled through clenched teeth, 'pack it in. People are staring.'

'But look,' he cried, 'they've got a *proper* laboratory. And have you seen the size of their canteen? And that sign up there says *IT Centre*. Not just a room like at school – a whole *centre*! I can't wait to be a university student. A *real* laboratory, *plus* parties all the time and making a lot of noise at three in the morning!'

The university was certainly an impressive place. A narrow road wandered through the main campus, passing all kinds of buildings, each of which was totally different in size and style to the ones either side. It looked as if teams of builders had raced each other to finish one idea after another. Signposts and diagrams pointed here, there and everywhere, to the Department of This-Subject and the Institute of That-Studies.

Muddy and I were surrounded by flowing streams of students, all of them way taller than us and most of them wearing designer jeans. By the time we found the Department of Mathematics, we'd heard nine languages being spoken and seen about a dozen contenders for Cool Dude of the Year.

'This is amaaaazing,' Muddy said, grinning.

The maths block was fronted by a large, paved area. In the middle of this plaza was a tall tree, its branches fanned out in an elegant dome, surrounded by a series of benches.

'You stay out here, Muddy,' I told him.

'Yes, sir,' said Muddy, parking himself on one of the benches.

'Pack it in. Seriously, don't go talking to anyone. I want to investigate incognito.'

'Wearing a what?' asked Muddy.

'No, incognito,' I said. 'It means "undercover", "on the quiet".'

'I bet Izzy told you that word,' muttered Muddy.

'Doesn't matter where I got the word,' I said, blushing slightly. 'Don't start talking to people about the case. I know what you're like. I don't want anyone knowing there's a brilliant schoolboy detective here. My enquiries are strictly off the record, so I don't need a blabbermouth like you asking questions. OK?'

'Yes, sir!' said Muddy, saluting.

'Oh, play with your camera or something,' I said crossly. I crossed the plaza and went into the maths building through sliding glass doors.

I found Dr Shroeder's study without any problem. It was on the ground floor, only a matter of metres away from the entrance. Right opposite the plaza I'd just left, in fact.

The corridor off which it stood was closed at the far end by heavy fire doors. On the right were various tutors' private offices. On the left, all along the corridor, were a series of wooden lockers and storage cupboards. These were roughly the same height as me. Above them, starting at about adult-shoulder level, were glistening windows, about a metre tall, which also ran from one end of the corridor to the other. They faced the plaza – I could see the top of that tree.

Pay attention to the layout of this corridor. It will become important later on!

I knocked on the door of Room 9B. I had no idea if Dr Shroeder was there or not, but I wanted to —

'Come in!' called a musical voice.

In I went. Dr Shroeder was a short, smiley man with

a patched-up corduroy jacket and hair which rose in huge, fuzzy grey tufts above his ears. His eyes blinked behind owlish spectacles and he flitted about from one thing to another like a hummingbird darting from flower to flower.

I introduced myself as a friend of a friend of Nat Hardyman. Dr Shroeder ushered me in and shook my hand enthusiastically.

'Delighted to meet you, young man,' he said. 'Come on in, can I get you a cup of tea? Or coffee? Or milk? Or lemon squash?'

'No, thanks, I'm fine.' I smiled.

'Thank goodness for that, I'm out of all of them,' said Dr Shroeder. 'Now then, you wanted to talk to me about poor Nat?'

I checked it was OK for me to record our conversation, and set Muddy's home-made recorder down on a workbench which ran along the wall beside the door. The room was a sort of half-classroom, half-office, with a large whiteboard at one end, a scattering of chairs and an assortment of bookcases and filing cabinets.

This is exactly what was said:

**Dr Shroeder:** Very sad business, about Hardyman.

Excellent student, I had high hopes for him.

**S Smart:** What exactly happened on Monday? I heard he came to see you?

**Dr Shroeder:** Yes, it must have been about, er, well, sometime after three in the afternoon. I'd just finished a class and he asked to speak to me privately. I thought it would be about the exam, or something like that, but he told me he took my computer.

**S Smart:** Did you believe him?

**Dr Shroeder:** I didn't want to, I must say. Most peculiar. I said to him, 'Nat, you're one of my brightest students, but everyone makes mistakes now and again. I'm prepared to put the whole matter down to a momentary lapse of judgement, a one-off giving-in to temptation. Return the computer and, just this once, nothing more will be said. I'll tell the principal's office I mislaid the laptop and have now found it, and that will be that.'

**S Smart:** That was kind of you. What did he say?

**Dr Shroeder:** Nothing, I'm afraid. In the end, I had no choice but to speak to the police. But something about Nat's manner convinced me that he was being forced into this strange confession. I was sure he didn't have the computer and so couldn't have returned it in any case.

S Smart: I got that impression, too. Does he have any enemies here?

Dr Shroeder: Enemies? No, definitely not. Nat is a quiet, studious boy. I don't think he has a wide social circle, but he certainly doesn't have enemies, as you put it. No, we have, let's see, thirty-eight students on the advanced maths curriculum, and they all get on very well, as far as I know.

S Smart: He told the police he took the computer to try to find the exam questions. Does that sound likely to you?

Dr Shroeder: No, that's utter nonsense. Rubbish. Poppycock. He'll sail through that exam. Or, rather, he would have sailed through it. Things look rather bleak for him at the moment. Frankly, I don't believe any of my current students would resort to cheating like that. They're all perfectly competent mathematicians. None of them needs to be worried about the exam. I'm confident they'll all achieve a pass. In any case, that computer had nothing on it about either the questions or the answers.

That information is perfectly safe.

**S Smart:** Can I ask you about the computer itself? It was almost new, wasn't it? A really trendy and expensive one?

**Dr Shroeder:** It was a Peartree SmartBook 400, yes. Not that I bought it because it's trendy, young man, I bought it because it's a powerful machine. Mind you, ah, it is rather smart, all white with nice silver trimming. And it has a beautifully curved design to the keyboard, which –

**S Smart:** Yes, I see. Er, so it's the sort of thing lots of students might be prepared to steal?

**Dr Shroeder:** Possibly, but a few of them have got one already.

**S Smart:** Really?

**Dr Shroeder:** Yes, I must have seen a dozen around the campus in the past couple of months. As you said yourself, they're trendy. No wonder some students get themselves into so much debt! I can tell what your next question is, and the answer is no. I haven't seen anyone new with one of those computers. There are even a couple of students on the advanced maths course who have them. In fact, it was having a look at a student's one - Debbie Ashworth's, I think it was - which prompted me to consider buying one for myself!

**S Smart:** So there'd be no way to distinguish your computer from any of the others that are around? If it actually turned up, I mean.

**Dr Shroeder:** Not looking at it from the outside, no. I fitted an extra hard drive into mine, as I need to store such a vast amount of data, but of course externally it looks identical to all the others.

**S Smart:** Well, I think that's all I need to ask. Thanks for your time, Dr Shroeder.

**Dr Shroeder:** Not at all, young man. I wish there was more I could do to help Nat Hardyman out. Ah! Look what I've found in this drawer! Tea bags! Would you like a cup of tea after all?

**S Smart:** Is that an unopened pack of chocolate biscuits I can see in there too?

**Dr Shroeder:** Oh yes, so it is. Help yourself.

**S Smart:** Yum!

I emerged from the maths building a few minutes later. What I expected to see was Muddy sitting quietly, on his own, maybe taking a snap or two with the Whitehouse

Snoop-o-Zoom Mark 2. What I actually saw was Muddy in the centre of a small crowd of students, laughing and joking and demonstrating the Whitehouse Snoop-o-Zoom Mark 2 to anyone who was interested.

I groaned to myself. I brushed the biscuit crumbs off my pullover and marched across to him.

'Muddyyyy,' I moaned. 'I said we had to be incognito!'

'Oh, hi Saxby,' he said. 'Hey, everyone, this is Saxby, the brilliant schoolboy detective I was telling you all about.'

'Hello Saxby!' cried everyone. There were about fifteen of them.

I slapped a hand to my forehead. 'Muddyyyyyyyy!'

'Most of these guys are on Nat's course,' said Muddy. 'Aren't you, guys?'

'Yeah,' nodded all the students.

'Pity he turned out to be a crook,' said one of them.

'When Nerds Go Bad . . .' said another in a doom-laden voice. That got a big laugh.

'I think it's awful what he did,' said a third. 'Dr Shroeder's been very good to all of us and look how Nat repays him.'

This third student, one of several girls in the group, caught my attention for two reasons. The first reason was that she was carrying one of those trendy laptops, the Rhubarb Crumble Thingummy 400, or whatever it was called. The second reason was that she was clearly a trendsetter in more than simply her choice of computer. I don't know how to describe fashions and similar girly stuff, but this student was obviously one who other girls imitated and who all the boys thought was cool. She was sleek and confident, all lips and hair.

'You're right, Debs,' said another girl. 'I hope they throw the book at that Nat.'

With calls of 'Bye, Muddy' and 'See ya, Muddy' and 'I'll bring that bike over for you to fix later, Muddy', the students went on their various ways.

'Y'know,' whispered Muddy to me, waving them goodbye, 'not one of that lot goes to parties all the time, *or* makes a lot of noise at three in the morning. Not *one*! I'm very disappointed.'

I watched the trendsetter disappear around a corner. 'There,' I said, mostly to myself, 'is a very, very pretty girl.'

Muddy snorted and nudged me in the ribs. 'Saxby's in luuuurve!'

'Shut yer face,' I grumbled. 'I was merely making an observation.'

'Well, you're not the only one,' said Muddy. 'Nat's in love with her too. Those students told me.'

'Eh?' I was about to moan at Muddy for talking to people about the case – exactly what I'd told him *not* to do. Then I realised he'd come across an interesting fact. So I shut up. Instead I said, 'Nat has a girlfriend?'

'Oh no, quite the opposite,' said Muddy. 'That girl is called Deborah Ashworth. She's Miss Popularity around here. Nat's madly in love with her, but she won't go out with him.'

'Why not?'

'She thinks he's a nerd,' said Muddy. 'Simple as that. He's not cool enough. I don't understand this yukky "love" business. I'm sticking to bike repairs when I grow up, I'm tellin' you.'

'Everyone knows Nat likes Deborah, then?' I said.

'Yes,' said Muddy. 'He's asked her out on dates several times, but she's always said no. She's also one of the best students on the advanced mathematics course.'

'Like Nat,' I said.

'Like Nat,' confirmed Muddy. 'He usually takes the top slot in tests and stuff, but she's very close behind him. And did you notice something?'

'What?'

'Did you see what she was carrying?'

'One of those computers,' I said. 'Like the one that was stolen. So?'

'So, there's a suspect for you!'

I sighed. 'No. She's had that laptop for a while. Definitely since before the theft.'

'How can you possibly know that?' gasped Muddy. 'You've never even seen her before.'

Look back at my chat with Dr Shroeder. Can you spot how I knew?

It was taking a look at Deborah Ashworth's computer that started Dr Shroeder thinking about buying one himself.

'I expect Deborah Ashworth is the sort of person who bought one of those laptops the day they arrived in the shops,' I said.

'She must be a better technician than me, you know,' said Muddy. 'One of those girls saw her accidentally spill nail polish into that laptop at the weekend and she's got it running fine now. I couldn't do that.'

'Forget nail polish,' I said. 'Tell me if there's anything else you've discovered.'

'Yes, there is one other thing,' said Muddy. 'Apparently, it's not unusual for students to call on Dr Shroeder before lessons start in the morning. He's told them that's the best time to find him in his office.'

'So,' I said, holding my chin in a detective-y way, 'the thief could well have been someone who called to see Dr Shroeder about some routine matter, but saw Dr Shroeder wasn't in his office for a few minutes, and so stole the computer on a kind of spur-of-the-moment impulse.'

'Er, yeah, that's just what I thought,' said Muddy. 'But there's more. Those students said it wasn't unusual for people to call on their tutor at that time of day, but it *was* unusual for them not to be seen.'

'How so?' I asked.

'Because there's usually more than one student wanting to see Dr Shroeder. The thief must have taken a huge risk, walking away with that laptop, because most days there'd be *another* student coming along any minute.'

'That's very interesting,' I muttered. I hopped to my feet. 'Right, now I must track down Nat's three friends . . .' I flipped back through my notebook, '. . . Matt, Jack and Anil. Good thing they weren't here with those others, I'd have been really mad. It's very important I get to speak to them separately *and* that they don't realise I'm investigating on behalf of Nat's mum. Very, very important.'

'Oh,' said Muddy quietly, pulling a whoops-a-daisy face.

I glared at him. He went red.

'What do you mean, "Oh"?' I murmured, eyes narrowed.

At that moment, three male students appeared. They walked around the corner of the maths building and headed directly for us.

'Sorry,' said Muddy with a sheepish grin. 'I got their numbers off my new student friends. I told them you wanted to speak to them urgently.'

'Muddyyyyyyyyyy!' I wailed.

All three of Nat's friends looked exactly like Nat:

carefully combed side partings, trousers slightly too short, glasses, plain zip-up cardigans. Was there some sort of geek uniform in this place?

'Are you the detective?' asked the tallest one, looking at Muddy.

'That would be me,' I said.

'I'm Matt,' said Matt.

'I'm Jack,' said Jack.

'I'm Anil,' said Anil.

'We've only come down here to say we're not going to talk to you,' said Matt. 'We've said all we've got to say, and we've said it to the cops. Goodbye.'

The three of them swung on their heels and marched away. I chased after them, Muddy scuttling along behind me. Matt, Jack and Anil were heading for the car park. I wrestled Muddy's recorder from my pocket and switched it on. This is what I managed to record:

S Smart: Wait! I only want to ask you some questions! I'm only trying to establish the truth!

Matt: Please go away.

Jack: We're very busy.

Anil: We've got essays to write.

S Smart: But don't you – [bumps into woman coming the other way] OOF! Sorry, beg your pardon!

Muddy: Don't you three want us to prove Nat

is innocent? You're his friends, aren't you?

**Matt:** Yeah, but he's guilty, isn't he?

**Anil:** Very sad, but there it is. We saw what we saw.

**S Smart** (swerving to avoid bashing into signpost): That's all I need to ask you about. What did you see? Exactly?

**Jack:** We've been through all this before. Go away.

**S Smart:** I've been told you saw him come out of Dr Shroeder's office holding the laptop. Is that true?

**Matt:** Yes. Now go away.

**S Smart:** All three of you saw that?

**Jack:** Yes.

**S Smart:** Where were you? Outside Dr Shroeder's office?

**Anil:** No, we were on those benches, where you were just sitting. We saw him clearly, through the window.

**S Smart:** All of you were there?

**Anil:** Yes. Go away.

**S Smart:** I'm asking because — [trips over edge of pavement] WHOAAA! Ow!

(Students arrive at car. Matt unlocks it. They get inside.)

**S Smart:** You're sure he was - ow, I've scraped my knee - he was carrying the laptop?

**Matt:** Yes, now will you get lost, you annoying little boy!

(Car door slams. Engine starts. Car drives off.)

Muddy and I watched Matt's battered old Ford chug and clunk its way out of the car park. I rubbed at my leg, wincing.

'Well, that didn't tell us anything,' sighed Muddy.

'Wrong,' I said. 'It proves they're lying. They've said they saw Nat coming out of Dr Shroeder's office with the laptop in his hands, yes?'

'Yes,' said Muddy.

'Well, they're lying.'

'How can you be sure?' said Muddy.

It was all a question of where they said they were, and the layout of that corridor outside Dr Shroeder's office. Can you work out why they must have lied?

(It's a tricky one – think carefully!)

They said they were sitting on the benches, in the plaza, outside the maths building. They said they saw, through the window, Nat come out of Dr Shroeder's office, and that Nat had the laptop with him.

But that can't be what they saw. Remember the layout of the corridor? Those windows that looked out on to the plaza? They were above those lockers and cupboards. They started at a level above my head, at an adult's shoulder level.

If someone was outside, looking in, all they could have seen coming out of Dr Shroeder's office was someone's head. (And if they were sitting on those benches, they might not have been able to see even that much – they might have only been able to see the top edge of the office door as it opened and closed!)

There was no way those three students could have seen anything Nat was or wasn't carrying. Well, unless he swung it around over his head. And that didn't seem very likely. So they had to be lying.

'And if they lied about that,' I said to Muddy, as we waited for the bus home, 'they probably lied about it all.'

'But that means they're deliberately trying to get their friend into trouble,' said Muddy. 'It doesn't make sense.'

'Nat's deliberately trying to get *himself* into trouble,'

I said. 'None of it makes sense.'

Little did I know, the answer to the entire problem would suddenly occur to me only a couple of hours later. In the meantime, I took out my notebook and jotted down a few thoughts.

# A Page From My Notebook

(Written on the bus - please excuse shaky handwriting.)

My visit to the university raises one or two new questions:

**QUESTION 1:** Could Nat have stolen the laptop to impress Deborah Ashworth? She thinks he's a nerd, nowhere near her level of trendiness. Could he have stolen the computer so that he too could walk around campus with one and look like a cool kid?

**WAIT!** No, no, no, that can't be right. Someone suddenly turning up with the same model of laptop as the stolen one would stick out a mile! AND that idea contradicts the fact that I now KNOW Nat's three friends have been lying.

**QUESTION 2:** Could Nat's FRIENDS have taken the computer? Could THEY be the ones bullying him into saying he did it? It would explain why they're lying.

**WAIT!** That can't be right either. Why would they make their FRIEND a scapegoat? And why would THEY steal the laptop? They wouldn't want the exam data (they're not studying maths), OR want to look trendy.

What am I MISSING here? Is there an element I've OVERLOOKED? Has Dr Shroeder told me the truth? Am I ever going to get my science homework finished?

# CHAPTER
## Five

MY PHONE RANG SHORTLY AFTER I got home. It was my other great friend Isobel 'Izzy' Moustique, and she had a favour to ask me.

'No,' I said.

'Aww, go on,' she pleaded. 'My mum will take us over to the cinema. But she's got a business meeting to get to, and I've got nobody to see the movie with.'

'See it on your own.'

'I don't want to see it on my own. Going to the movies is something you do with friends.'

'Well ask a friend who isn't me,' I said.

'I already have,' grumbled Izzy. 'They're all busy. You're right at the bottom of my list.'

'Nice.'

'Aww, go on. Might be the best film you've ever seen.'

'What's it called?' I asked, suspiciously.

'*Blood Beasts of Mars.*'

'See you in ten minutes.'

*At least it'll take my mind off the Hardyman case*, I thought. *At least it sounds like it'll have plenty of monsters and battles in it, I thought. Maybe even a car chase or two.*

Wrong. It was a weedy love story about an earthling who looks after a wounded alien, full of weepy violin music and sunsets and yuueeek bleaghh euikkkk!

'That is the most misleading movie title in the history of movies!' I moaned, as we left the cinema. 'You *knew* it was going to be like that, didn't you?'

Izzy pulled an exaggerated who-li'l-ol'-me? face. 'But it was so *moving* —'

'Yawn!'

'So *romantic* —'

'Double yawn!'

'He gave up his life as a space marine,' sighed Izzy, 'so that they could be in each other's arms. Well, tentacles, anyway. Ahhhhh! Oh, there's the car, I can see Mum waving.'

Wait a minute.

'Say that again,' I said.

'I said I can see the car,' replied Izzy.

'No, before that . . . Good grief, that's the answer!'

I hadn't wasted two hours of my life sitting through that rubbish movie after all. Suddenly, I had the key to the whole Hardyman mystery! It revolved around three vital elements:

1. *Blood Beasts of Mars*,

2. Dr Shroeder needing a wee last Monday morning, and

3. A bottle of nail polish.

How much of the puzzle have you pieced together?

At nine a.m. the following morning, eight people gathered in Dr Shroeder's office at the university – there was me, Dr Shroeder, Nat Hardyman and his mum, Deborah Ashworth, Matt, Jack and Anil. I'd also asked Dr Shroeder if he could invite along whichever police officer it was who'd dusted for fingerprints on the morning of the theft. But they hadn't arrived yet.

'What's this about?' said Deborah Ashworth. 'I've got an exam to revise for. Why aren't the rest of the advanced maths group here?'

'Everything will be clear in a few minutes,' I said.

'I'm not even supposed to be on campus,' said Nat. 'The head of department said I was banned until further notice.'

'You won't be for much longer,' I reassured him. He didn't look reassured one little bit. If anything, he looked extremely nervous and uncomfortable.

'Perhaps you could get on with saying whatever it is you've called us here to say?' suggested Dr Shroeder.

'OK,' I began. I a-hemmed, feeling rather nervous myself.

I was taking a leap in the dark. I had good reasons for thinking that my deductions were correct, but there were still some parts of the mystery I couldn't be certain about. If I was wrong, if I'd made a mistake in my investigations, I was about to make myself look like a complete and utter idiot.

'OK,' I began again. 'I'll start by saying that Nat Hardyman, whatever he might say, and whatever his three friends here might say, is innocent of the crime.'

I could see that Nat was about to say 'No, I'm not', but then thought better of it. He glanced around the room, at the others, then dropped his gaze to the floor.

'So who *is* guilty, then?' said Dr Shroeder.

'We need to reconstruct what happened last Monday morning,' I said. 'You arrived here, Dr Shroeder, at your office, as you normally would. You got out your new computer, but then you realised you needed to go to the loo. So off you went.

'Students often call to see you at that time in the morning. Monday was no exception. While you were gone, a student turned up. You weren't here. Now, under normal circumstances, they might simply have waited for you to return. Or they might have come back later. But on Monday, that student spotted an unexpected opportunity and gave in to a sudden temptation. They picked up your computer and walked out with it.'

'Yes, it was Nat,' said Matt.

'No,' I said. 'It wasn't Nat. But Nat was here. Or rather, Nat was outside, in the corridor. By chance, he'd also come along to see Dr Shroeder. What it was about, I don't know. I don't know what the thief originally came here to ask either, but I guess that's something that can wait until later.

'Nat happened to come through the door at the end of the corridor, just as the thief was leaving this room. He saw who it was. He saw the guilty look on the thief's face, he saw the laptop, and he remembered something he'd just heard a fellow student mention.

'At this point, I should say, I'm having to make one or two logical leaps. I don't know how Nat heard what he heard a fellow student mention. He'll have to tell us that himself.'

'So who was this thief?' said Deborah Ashworth. 'I think we'd all like to know.'

I paused for a moment. 'All the way through this investigation,' I said, 'I've been wondering who could possibly have forced Nat to admit to a crime he didn't commit. And after I saw a really soppy film yesterday, the truth suddenly dawned on me. The truth is, he forced himself.'

'Himself?' said Mrs Hardyman. 'How? He's such a good boy. Are you saying he bullied himself into a false confession?'

'Not exactly,' I said. 'As you've said, Mrs Hardyman, Nat's never been in trouble in his life. He's not exactly used to hatching plots, so he did it all rather clumsily.

His aim was to stop the thief being found out. He was willing to get into serious trouble and risk his entire future to protect that person.'

'Protect who?' gasped Dr Shroeder.

'Do you want to tell them, Nat?' I said. 'Or shall I? She knows what you've done and she doesn't seem to care. She'll let you take the blame. You owe her nothing.'

Nat shifted uneasily. A couple of times, he seemed about to speak. At last he said, in a faltering voice, 'No. I won't say anything.'

'Who is this "she"?' said Dr Shroeder. 'Who is he protecting?'

I waited a few seconds. Just in case she felt like doing the right thing and owning up. Hmm, apparently she didn't.

'Deborah Ashworth,' I said.

She hooted with laughter. 'Oh, that's ridiculous. Why would I steal Dr Shroeder's laptop? I've got an identical one myself!'

'You *did* have,' I said. 'At the weekend, you accidentally tipped nail polish into it.'

'I fixed it!' Deborah protested.

'According to my friend, Muddy, that would be very difficult. Beyond his capabilities. And, to be quite honest, if something technical is beyond my friend Muddy, it's beyond just about everyone. Yet, apparently, you not only fixed it, you fixed it almost overnight.'

Deborah pulled the laptop from a bag at her feet. 'This is my computer. There's no way you can prove otherwise.'

'Wait, I don't understand,' said Mrs Hardyman. 'Why would Nat cover up for this girl?'

'Because he loves her,' I said. 'That's where we come back to that soppy film I saw yesterday. Some people will do the craziest things for love. In this case, Nat was willing to be thrown out of university, maybe even end up with a police record, to show Deborah how much he loves her. He thought he might be able to change her mind about him. He thought that, just maybe, she'd stop thinking of him as a nerd if he did something like that for her sake, and that she might fall in love with him too.'

'Nat?' said Mrs Hardyman in a quiet voice. 'Is this true?'

Nat seemed to be looking in every possible direction at once, except at us. He ran his hands through his neatly combed hair, pulling at it sharply.

'Outside this building,' he said, barely above a whisper, 'on Monday morning, I was talking to a couple of the girls on my course about what we'd done at the weekend. One of them told me about Debbie's accident with her computer. I knew it couldn't have been fixed. When I came inside, as soon as I saw the one under her arm, I knew it had to be Dr Shroeder's.'

'That's a lie,' said Deborah sharply.

'She looked at me,' said Nat sadly. 'Straight at me. Both of us knew what was going on, just from each other's faces. I said, "I won't tell." She walked away.'

I looked across at Nat's three friends. They looked almost as agonised as Nat himself.

'So why did these three back up his story?' cried Mrs Hardyman. 'Some friends they are!'

'They backed up his story *because* they're his friends,' I said. 'He asked them to.'

'I told you it was a stupid idea, Nat,' grumbled Matt. 'I said it wouldn't work.'

'Nat thought that, if he went to the police and owned up to the crime, then he'd be charged and that would be that,' I said. 'But once again, Mrs Hardyman, because he's a good boy who's never been in trouble in his life, he didn't realise that the police would want more than a simple confession.

'So, after they let him go late on Monday, he called his three friends from home. He asked them to come forward as witnesses. And so, on Tuesday morning, bingo, out of the blue, there were suddenly three people backing up Nat's version of events. My guess is that they were very reluctant to go along with Nat's idea – as shown by the way they didn't want to talk to anyone but the police about it – but they did it out of loyalty to their friend. They knew how much Nat loves Deborah.'

'And we told him she wouldn't care,' said Anil. 'The girl's got a heart of stone.'

'Listen,' cried Deborah, 'this is all lies. This computer belongs to me!'

'We've no way of proving otherwise,' said Dr Shroeder. 'Miss Ashworth has had one of these laptops for a while. I can't see that there would be any difference between mine and hers.'

'Oh yes there is,' I said. 'Miss Ashworth, would you put the computer on this workbench and raise its screen?'

Deborah glared at the rest of us for a moment, then with a huff and a shake of her head she did as I asked. 'There! Happy?'

'Thanks,' I said. 'Now, could you pull the two little catches that hold the keyboard in place and lift it out?'

'What for?' she said.

'To prove whose computer this really is,' I said. 'Umm, Dr Shroeder, is that police officer going to get here soon?'

'I don't know,' said Dr Shroeder. 'She said she'd be along as soon as possible.'

Making a show of how good she was being by co-operating, Deborah lifted the computer's keyboard, exposing a hole through which the machine's innards could be seen.

'Happy now?' she said, frostily. 'Standard components.'

'Not quite,' I said. 'If everybody could make sure they don't actually touch the computer now? Thank you.'

I'd thought of a good way to demonstrate that this was indeed Dr Shroeder's computer, based on something he'd told me the day before.

Have you spotted it?

'Dr Shroeder,' I said, 'you know more about these things than I do. Could you point out where the hard drive is?'

Dr Shroeder frowned slightly, puzzled by my request. 'It's the small silver box on the right-hand side. The one with a white label on it. But why?'

'Do you remember what you told me yesterday?' I said.

Suddenly, Dr Shroeder snapped his fingers and grinned. 'I told you I'd upgraded the hard drive! Yes, I see! The thief wouldn't have known that. *That* drive there *is* the exact model I installed.'

'Me too,' said Deborah flatly. 'I also installed the same upgrade.'

'You did? Yourself?' I said.

'Yes,' snapped Deborah.

'You didn't get Dr Shroeder to do it for you?'

'Of course not!'

'OoooKaaaay,' I said. 'So, when this police officer gets here . . . finally . . . we'll be able to find out whose fingerprints are on that drive. If this is your computer, Deborah, then they'll be your prints.'

Deborah took a step back. Then another step. I knew she was going to make a run for it. I just knew. As soon as she bolted for the door, Mrs Hardyman was after her.

'Oi! Get back here! I'll teach you to break my boy's

heart, you nasty piece of work!'

When they'd gone, Dr Shroeder turned to me. 'Why did she do it? She's such a good student, why would she steal my computer?'

I shrugged. 'Just to replace her own. Just so she wouldn't look like a twit for ruining her expensive gear. Just so she could stay looking cool, with one of those trendy machines under her arm.'

'Astonishing,' said Dr Shroeder. 'What motivated her was so feeble and shallow, and yet what motivated Nat was the strongest emotion in the world, a force powerful enough to overcome his reason, his common sense, his rational thought.'

'I am still in the room,' muttered Nat.

'Come on, mate,' said Matt, patting Nat on the back. 'We'll all go over to my place. I've just got *Star Trek* on Blu-ray.'

He followed them out of the office, looking as miserable and bedraggled as a small furry animal that's just fought its way out of a flushing toilet.

Dr Shroeder sighed. 'You can't choose who you love,' he said.

The police officer arrived at Dr Shroeder's office a couple of hours later, by which time I was back at my garden shed. She was able to confirm that Dr Shroeder's fingerprints were on the hard drive. (Thank goodness. If they'd turned out to be Deborah's, I don't know what I'd have done!)

Nat was reinstated on to the advanced mathematics course the following day, at about the same time as Deborah Ashworth was being questioned by the police. Once the situation at school was back to normal, Mrs Hardyman started giving me extra dollops of vegetable stew whenever she saw me in the dinner queue. I'd much rather have had an extra dollop of the chocolate pudding, but I guess she was just trying to be kind.

Meanwhile, back at my garden shed, I flopped into my Thinking Chair and vowed that I would *never* let my heart rule my head. Dr Shroeder had been absolutely right about Nat's motive.

And this is where we get back to the point I was making way back at the start of Chapter One. Remembering all the crime stories I'd read, I was reminded that Sherlock Holmes had one or two things to say about love. Mostly rather grumpy things, I seem to recall. Emotions are funny things, certainly when it came to Nat Hardyman's motive.

I simply hadn't seen it because I was concentrating on my role as a detective, on staying logical. Sometimes, I said to myself, I guess you have to take account of the illogical and the intuitive as well.

I jotted down some notes and sat in my Thinking Chair mulling over the strange and peculiar things that grown-ups do. It was only later on, as I placed my notes into my filing cabinet, that I realised I still hadn't done my science homework.

Oh poo.

Case closed.

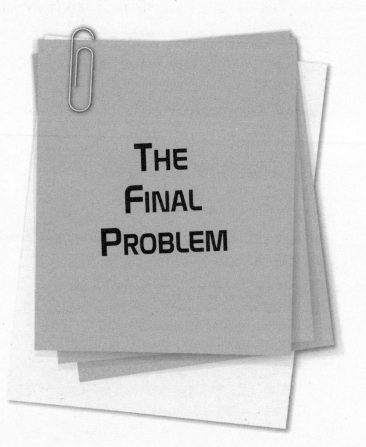

# THE
# FINAL
# PROBLEM

# CHAPTER ONE

I *MEANT* TO GET MY science homework done on time. I really did. But I got distracted.

I was in my garden shed, or my Crime HQ as I prefer to call it. I had my science homework open on the desk. I'd read through the questions carefully and I had my pen poised over my workbook, ready to begin.

And then there was a knock at the shed door.

For the tiniest fraction of a nano-second, I thought about pretending I wasn't in. This science homework needed doing and it needed doing right now. But when you're a brilliant schoolboy detective, like me, a simple knock on the door can mean the start of something *big*.

Hmm. Science homework, or the possibility of an important new investigation? Hmmmmmm . . .

'Come in!' I cried.

Two people entered the shed. The first was my great friend Isobel 'Izzy' Moustique, that well-known genius and St Egbert's School's Commander-in-Chief of All Research Data, whose talent for finding information has played a vital part in many of my case files.

The second was Jeremy Sweetly, a boy who's also in my class at school, and who happens to live across the street from me. He's a nice guy and we all like him, but he's a bit . . . weeeeeell, I don't want to sound unkind, but . . . he's a bit weedy. A bit wet. A bit of a drip. (I'd helped him during my case file *The Mark of the Purple Homework*.) I was relieved to see that he hadn't brought his horrible great slobbery dog Humphrey with him. I hate that dog.

'Hello, you two,' I said. 'What can I do for you?'

'We've got a bit of a problem,' trembled Jeremy.

Izzy noticed the workbook on the desk. 'Oh, you're doing your science homework. We'll come back later.'

'No, that's OK, come on in,' I said, gratefully flipping the workbook shut.

Jeremy gasped. 'Haven't you finished your science homework yet?'

'No,' I said.

Jeremy gasped again. 'That should have been done ages ago.'

'Yes,' I said.

'Aren't you worried you'll be in trouble?' He gawped at me like a startled goldfish.

'Yes, no, yes, oh I dunno,' I grumbled. 'Anyway, tell me about this problem.'

'You tell him,' said Jeremy to Izzy. 'I'm still too upset to get it straight in my head.'

Izzy, who was wearing her usual out-of-school gear (brightly coloured everything with added glitter), flicked a hanky across my desk to dust it down.

'What's the matter with boys?' she muttered. 'All live in pigsties.' She parked herself on the desk and turned to me.

'Jeremy and I are half of the St Egbert's team in the Brain Boom Schools Quiz Challenge,' she said. She tutted and shook her head. 'Sorry, I'm forgetting, you already know that.'

'Oh yes,' I said. 'I definitely already know that.'

The whole of St Egbert's School definitely already knew that. Izzy and Jeremy, along with two kids from Mr Nailshott's class, had been specially picked for the team. The Brain Boom Schools Quiz Challenge was a general knowledge knockout competition that some-education-department-or-other was running with one of the nearby radio stations, Vibe FM.

They'd started with sixteen schools. The St Egbert's

team had battled their way through three rounds and had now qualified for the grand final. (Round one had been quite tricky, but Izzy and co had absolutely wiped the floor with their opponents in the quarter-finals, while the semi-finals had been a real nail-chewer.)

Our team was the Head's pride and joy at the moment. She seemed to be spending all day skipping up and down the corridors and accidentally-on-purpose mentioning the team to visitors and reminding Izzy and co to eat plenty of fresh fish and get enough sleep.

'So, when's the grand final?' I asked.

Izzy and Jeremy glared at me, pop-eyed. 'Don't tell me you haven't been listening to it all on the radio?' grumbled Izzy.

'I heard the ones you two were in, obviously,' I said, 'but I've been very busy working on a case. I thought I might write it up as *The Adventure of the Twisted Sparrow*.'

'The grand final is this Saturday afternoon,' said Izzy. 'All the heats have taken place at different schools; the final is being held in our school's main hall and it's going out on the radio live.'

'The twisted what?' muttered Jeremy to himself.

'Weren't all the other rounds live?' I asked.

'No,' said Izzy. 'All the heats have been pre-recorded at the schools. The recordings were being broadcast every weeknight in the three weeks running up to this

Saturday. But the half-hour final goes out live at five o'clock.'

'Who are you up against?' I said.

'That's why we've come to see you, Saxby,' shivered Jeremy. 'St Egbert's are facing Spykeside School.'

'Never heard of it,' I said.

'Neither had we until we started the competition,' said Jeremy. 'The place is miles away. But unless you help us, Spykeside are going to win.'

'Er, well, that's very flattering,' I said, 'but, er, don't forget that my maths isn't exactly —'

'Noooo, you dummy!' interrupted Izzy. 'We don't need your help on the *team*! We need your help because Spykeside School have been *cheating*!'

# CHAPTER
# TWO

'CHEATING?' I SAID. 'HOW DO you know?'

'They've won every time so far,' said Jeremy.

'Well, so have *you*,' I pointed out. 'That's why both schools are in the final! Surely they're just good at answering general knowledge questions?'

'*Before* they're even asked?' said Izzy.

'Huh?' I said.

'It's not very noticeable until you listen carefully for it, because the questions are very quick-fire,' explained Izzy. 'But it's like this: each team has a buzzer, right? First team to buzz gets first go at answering, right? Several times, Spykeside have buzzed before that twerpy DJ who's asking the questions has even finished.'

'Lucky guesses?' I said. 'You see that sometimes on

quiz shows. People can sometimes correctly anticipate the question.'

'Forty-three times?' said Izzy. 'Once we started getting suspicious, I went back and checked. I counted. Don't forget, Spykeside have been in exactly the same number of heats as we have. That's forty-three times in three half-hour quizzes they've pressed their buzzer before the end of the question. And thirteen of those times, they pressed the buzzer before you could sensibly anticipate what the question was going to be. Like I said, it's actually quite easy to miss unless you're listening out for it, because of the speed of the questions.'

'It could still be that they're simply very, very bright,' I said.

'OK,' said Izzy. 'Here's an example. Answer this question: Who was the third actor . . . ?'

I stared at her. 'The third actor who what?' I asked.

'Exactly,' said Izzy.

'That's when Spykeside buzzed,' said Jeremy. 'And they got it right. Roger Moore. Who was the third actor to play James Bond in the official movie series?'

I thought for a moment, hmmmm-ing and wrinkling my nose. 'I guess they *could* still have worked it out,' I said. 'After all, the words "third actor" narrow down possible answers to just a handful. If three actors have all played one part, then it must be an unusually successful and long-running part. And how many of those are there? Saying "James Bond" could have been an answer based on weighing up the limited possibilities and some very fast thinking.'

Jeremy muttered, 'It might have been: Who was the third actor to get swept out to sea by a giant squid at last year's Dorset Film Festival?'

I pulled an oh-yeahhh-right face at him. 'I don't think that's very likely, do you?'

'OK, answering a barely-asked question once or twice *could* be down to very fast thinking,' said Izzy. 'But *thirteen* times? Try these three:

'Question one: In what year did the first [BUZZ!] . . .?

'Question two: In which play by Shakespeare does the main character say [BUZZ!] . . .?

'Question three: At what temperature does [BUZZ!] . . .?

'Spykeside had answered them all correctly.'

Hmmmmm.

What do you think? Can you work out the answers? Did Spykeside cheat?

I scratched my head. Then I scratched my chin. Then I scratched my nose. Once I'd run out of things to scratch, I said, 'No idea. What year was the first sausage roll made? In which Shakespeare play does someone say "Hey dude, check out my cool new trainers"? At what temperature does our form tutor Mrs Penzler explode? Those questions could refer to anything.'

'So you can't answer them?' said Izzy.

'Well, the last one might be about the boiling point of water, maybe?'

'Close,' said Izzy. 'It was about the freezing point of water.'

'Zero degrees centigrade,' said Jeremy.

'I know that!' I said.

'Sorry,' mumbled Jeremy. 'Y'know, if you haven't done your science homework yet . . .'

'I have to admit,' I said, 'it looks very much like Spykeside *did* know what the questions were going to be. They *did* cheat. What were the other answers?'

'The first one was 1969. In what year did the first man land on the moon? The second was *Hamlet*. In which play by Shakespeare does the main character say "To be or not to be"?'

'You're right,' I said, 'the odds of correctly guessing the answers over and over again would be pretty slim. But maybe that's simply their strategy for playing? Buzz in quick and take a guess, just to stop the other team from answering first?'

Izzy and Jeremy both groaned.

'Did you even listen to the heats *we* were in?' said Izzy.

'Yes!' I cried. 'Well, I had the radio on while I was working on some case notes.'

'Spykeside can't be using a "buzz in quick" strategy,' said Izzy, 'because you lose a point if you get the answer wrong. It's two points for a right answer, minus one point for a wrong answer. If they were just making guesses they'd end up with a negative score!'

'Ah, right, yes, I remember now,' I said hurriedly, 'a-hem, yes, a-hem. So what made you suspicious about the Spykeside team in the first place? Did they say something to you?'

'No, none of the St Egbert's team has ever met them,' said Jeremy.

'Because it's a knockout competition,' said Izzy, 'there are several teams we've not played, and by the luck of the draw Spykeside are one of them. The grand final on Saturday is the first and only time we'll get to meet them. We became suspicious simply by listening to the other heats, and to the way Spykeside kept jumping in with correct answers. After that, I asked around to see if anyone I knew had any contacts at Spykeside. Nobody had, but one of my cousins [Izzy has loads of cousins. Loads. Several hundred, you'd think, judging from the way her network of cousins was always able to come up trumps.] was at one of the earlier recordings, over at a school near Birmingham. She never got to talk to any of them, but she said they looked like a bunch of rejects from a gangster movie.'

'Do we know their names?' I asked.

'Unfortunately not,' said Izzy. 'For the competition the Spykeside team are using aliases: Superguy, Captain Cool, the Brainiator and Mr Electron.'

'Oh *yuk*!' I snorted.

'Dreadful, right?' said Izzy. 'But the radio station seem to think it's cute, so they're playing along. The official Brain Boom Schools Quiz Challenge website includes photos of most of the teams, but Spykeside isn't included. Spykeside School's own website doesn't even mention the quiz – I don't think it's been updated for about two years.'

I adopted a detective-style, deep-thinking expression. 'That's very odd,' I said. 'It's almost as if they're trying to hide their identities.'

'They're also being very clever about this whole cheating business,' said Izzy. 'They never overdo it. The cheating only becomes noticeable once you start listening for it. They keep letting the other team get ahead, but then before the end of the quiz they slowly overtake on points with a steady run of correct answers. And now and again they answer a question with a wildly wrong answer, so it looks like they're in a panic.'

'Interesting,' I muttered. 'There are some genuine brains at work there, then. Who's setting the quiz questions?'

'Someone at Vibe FM,' said Jeremy. 'We think it's probably the DJ who's being the quizmaster.'

'And the *big* question,' I said, 'the one we've not mentioned so far, is: Why cheat? What's first prize in this competition?'

'The winning school gets a thousand pounds for their library,' said Izzy. 'Each member of the winning team gets a hundred pounds in book vouchers, plus a hundred free music downloads from Vibe FM, plus a one-year free pass to every theme park and tourist attraction that's worth going to.'

'Not bad,' I said. 'I guess that lot's worth cheating for, then. What we need to work out is —'

At that moment, we all heard a distinct scratching noise coming from outside the shed. We froze, listening.

It was a sharp, scraping sound. Someone was beside the door, out of sight of the shed's perspex window.

Izzy leaned over to me and whispered, 'I think we've been followed.'

I nodded. Jeremy stood there looking terrified.

Slowly, trying to make sure I didn't creak any floorboards, I crept over to the door. I put my shoulder to it, ready to fling it open and catch whoever-it-was before they could escape.

Had our conversation been overheard? Had the Spykeside team sent someone to spy on us?

I looked back at Izzy. Three . . . Two . . . One . . . *Go!*

I crashed open the shed door and bounded outside. I was going to shout '*A-ha! Caught you!*' but what I actually shouted was 'Whoaaaaa!'

I tripped over a solid mass that was lurking beside the door and went head over heels onto the garden lawn. I spun around. I found myself staring into the wrinkly, snuffly face of Jeremy's huge slobbery dog, Humphrey.

'Jeremy!' I yelled, as that great drooling hound came lolloping towards me. 'He's got out again! Help! Heeeeelp!'

Jeremy caught Humphrey by the collar and started going all huggy cuddly over his wuvvwy poochie-poo. Made me feel ill.

'Can't you keep him under control?' I grumbled, scrambling to my feet before Humphrey could start dribbling on me. 'That dog escapes and comes looking for you every five minutes!'

'He's a cwevvver doggie, aren't you, humphy-wumphy,' said Jeremy.

I hate that dog.

# A Page From My Notebook

It seems fairly clear that Spykeside ARE cheating. Either that or they've got the ability to look a few seconds into the future, see what questions are coming up and then know how to answer them perfectly . . . Hmm. No, they're cheating.

**QUESTION:** HOW are they cheating? If it's a case of knowing the questions in advance, then . . .

**ANSWER 1:** They're STEALING the questions before each quiz.
**OR ANSWER 2:** They're BEING GIVEN the questions before each quiz.

If ANSWER 1 is correct, then HOW are they doing it? If ANSWER 2 is correct, then WHO is helping them? (Someone at Vibe FM, presumably.) And WHY? (Why would Vibe FM want to fix the result of the competition?)

**WAIT!** POSSIBLE ALTERNATIVE CHEATING METHOD! Could it be that the Spykeside team have discovered WHERE Vibe FM are getting the questions from (a particular online encyclopedia, something like that), and are using that same source of info to learn facts from? In other words, could it be that they're NOT getting the actual questions in advance, but simply studying the SOURCE of the questions (whether it's a book, an online database, or whatever)?

**WAIT!** Hang on, no. That's not possible. It means they'd have to LEARN that entire encyclopedia. Which means they'd have to have the world's best memories. Which means they'd have no need to cheat!

No, they MUST be getting the actual questions in advance.

What should be the next step in my investigation?

**PLAN A:** Ideally, I need to talk to someone at Spykeside School. However, from what Izzy and Jeremy have told me, that's unlikely to be possible. Is there any way I could go undercover at Spykeside myself? That seems even less likely. I'd be rumbled instantly.

**PLAN B:** The first thing I must do is listen to those other radio shows. There may be some more clues to be picked up.

# Chapter
# Three

I SPENT THE EVENING LOGGED on to the Hear It Again page
of Vibe FM's website, listening to all the quiz heats I'd
missed and making notes. (I tried answering the
questions myself as I went along. After only seven heats
I'd amassed the same number of correct answers as the
St Egbert's team had scored in their first round. I was
quite pleased with myself.)

Once I'd finished, I could see exactly why Izzy and
Jeremy had become suspicious of the Spykeside team.
The questions were pretty rapid-fire, so it was easy to
miss the fact that Spykeside were anticipating questions
rather too regularly. However, once I'd clicked the
rewind button here and there and listened carefully, I
could spot the remarkable snappiness of their answers to

questions like that 'Who was the third actor . . .' one.

I'd also spotted something else – something Izzy and the rest of the St Egbert's team hadn't. Here are some figures I jotted down as I listened to the three heats Spykeside had taken part in so far: Do you notice something about the Spykeside team?

| Round 1 Questions | | | |
|---|---|---|---|
| Teams and Player | Right | Wrong | Points |
| Spykeside (total) | 42 | 4 | 80 |
| Superguy | 11 | 1 | 21 |
| Capt. Cool | 19 | 2 | 36 |
| Mr Electron | 0 | 0 | 0 |
| The Brainiator | 12 | 1 | 23 |
| Opponents (total) | 19 | 9 | 29 |
| Team Member 1 | 4 | 3 | 5 |
| Team Member 2 | 7 | 0 | 14 |
| Team Member 3 | 7 | 2 | 12 |
| Team Member 4 | 1 | 4 | (-2) |

## Quarter-Final Questions

| Teams and Player | Right | Wrong | Points |
|---|---|---|---|
| Spykeside (total) | 33 | 6 | 60 |
| Superguy | 10 | 2 | 18 |
| Capt. Cool | 12 | 2 | 22 |
| Mr Electron | 0 | 0 | 0 |
| The Brainiator | 11 | 2 | 20 |
| Opponents (total) | 27 | 11 | 43 |
| Team Member 1 | 13 | 0 | 26 |
| Team Member 2 | 6 | 0 | 12 |
| Team Member 3 | 0 | 11 | (-11) |
| Team Member 4 | 8 | 4 | 16 |

## Semi-Final Questions

| Teams and Player | Right | Wrong | Points |
|---|---|---|---|
| Spykeside (total) | 38 | 5 | 71 |
| Superguy | 13 | 2 | 24 |
| Capt. Cool | 13 | 2 | 24 |
| Mr Electron | 0 | 0 | 0 |
| The Brainiator | 12 | 1 | 23 |
| Opponents (total) | 30 | 12 | 48 |
| Team Member 1 | 3 | 2 | 4 |
| Team Member 2 | 10 | 3 | 17 |
| Team Member 3 | 9 | 3 | 15 |
| Team Member 4 | 8 | 4 | 12 |

There was one member of the Spykeside team – this Mr Electron person – who hadn't answered a single question, either right or wrong. (Also, you could see that Spykeside's quarter-final opponents had one really rubbish team member. But that's not relevant to the case. I'm just pointing it out.)

Listening to those quizzes, it was clear that this Mr Electron person hadn't so much as *spoken*.

Weird.

At school the next day – Friday – I sat next to Izzy at lunchtime. I told her about my discovery.

'Weird,' she said.

'Your cousin,' I said, 'the one who saw one of the earlier heats being recorded. She didn't mention anything about this Mr Electron person, did she? I mean, the team isn't three people and a knitted mascot or something?'

'No,' said Izzy. 'Definitely four Spykeside pupils.'

'So why would they have one member of the team who never says anything?'

Izzy shrugged. 'Maybe he's very shy. Or a bit dim.'

'But they're *cheating*,' I said. 'They all know the answers.'

'Perhaps he's the only one in the team who *isn't* cheating?' said Izzy. 'Perhaps he's found out what's going on and the others have shut him up?'

'That's possible, I suppose,' I mumbled. 'Or perhaps he's decided to say nothing and walk away with the prizes like the rest of them. I wish we could get a look at these guys.'

Izzy almost leaped out of her seat. 'That reminds me! I did a lot more searching last night and I found a photo. A very bad one, but it's better than nothing.'

From her school bag she produced a website printout. Sandwiched in between a couple of short articles and a fringe of adverts, there was a small, rather dark picture.

'I got this from a local news site that covers Spykeside,' said Izzy. 'It was only posted a couple of days ago. That's why I didn't find anything last time I looked.'

Under the photo was a paragraph which read:

*The head teacher of Spykeside School, Mr Bradley Mole, poses with the team who have made it through to the final of the Brain Boom Schools Quiz Challenge: (left to right) Captain Cool, Superguy, the Brainiator and Mr Electron.*

The head teacher looked like he'd recently arisen from the grave, and the Spykeside team were (left to right) three bug-eyed uglies and a fuzzy blur. The Brainiator was a bruiser who looked like he'd eaten a bag of nails for breakfast. And then eaten another bag of nails, just to show how tough he was.

'What a bunch,' I whistled. 'Do you suppose this was taken in a distorting mirror? I can only *hope* this was taken in a distorting mirror.'

'There's the silent Mr Electron on the right,' said Izzy. 'He must have moved his head just as the picture was taken.'

I held the paper up close to my nose. I squinted a bit, and angled the picture into the sunlight that was flooding through the dining hall windows, but nothing revealed any further details.

'I wonder,' I said, 'if this Mr Electron person doesn't want to be heard, perhaps he doesn't want to be seen either.'

'You think he's trying to stay anonymous?' asked Izzy.

'I think the whole team is trying to stay as anonymous as possible,' I replied. 'But this Mr Electron person is keeping himself positively invisible. Can I keep this picture?'

'Sure.'

'I think I'll take it over to Muddy's lab after school. He might have some gizmo which will get us a better look at it.'

My great friend George 'Muddy' Whitehouse was St

Egbert's School's unofficial Head of Technical Wizardry. Anything he didn't know about the world of gadgets probably wasn't worth knowing.

Later that day, while Izzy was digging around for any more information which might be useful, I went to see Muddy in the garage attached to his house – or his Development Laboratory, as he prefers to call it. He was busy adapting a couple of old bikes into a go-cart. As always, his school uniform was littered with an assortment of oil stains, food stains and plain old-fashioned grime. He wiped his greasy hands on his shirt before taking Izzy's printout from me.

'Is this the best photo you can find?' he said, scrunching up his face to peer closely at it.

'I'm afraid so,' I said.

'Brilliant!' he declared. 'It'll give me a chance to try out the Whitehouse OptiScope Mark 3.'

He clattered his way through the debris of odds and ends which half-filled his lab. Clearing a space on his workbench by sweeping a load of electrical components off it with his sleeve, he placed the photo down, face up.

'Any definite leads yet?' he said, while he rooted around for various gizmos.

'No, not really,' I said. 'Half the problem is that Spykeside School is miles away and I've got no way of investigating the place. And the other half of the problem is that I'm stumped.'

Muddy set up a kind of tripod around the printout, at the top of which he fixed something that might once have been a camera. Or possibly an electric whisk.

'Put this together from half a pair of binoculars and the innards of my dad's phone,' said Muddy, making a few delicate adjustments. 'Designed to catch fast-moving action at sports events. Only it takes a while to set up, so it's not very good for that. If I fiddle with the lens, we should be able to see the picture much more clearly. So, you've no real clues, as such?'

'Weeellll,' I said, a bit embarrassed, 'I'm, y'know, keeping an open mind and, umm, y'know . . .'

'That bad, huh?' He tapped a tiny screen on the side of the device and it flickered into life. He started pressing a few buttons.

'There is one thing I'm sure of,' I said. 'The way the Spykeside team are hiding behind nicknames is significant. They're a funny-looking bunch, as you can see from that picture, and they're being very sneaky about their cheating methods. But without knowing who any of them are, it's very hard to work out what to do next. We know they're getting hold of the quiz questions in advance, but since we have no way of identifying any of them —'

Muddy suddenly turned and looked at me. Even under the layer of dirt on his face, I could tell he'd gone pale with horror.

'No way of identifying them?' he said quietly. 'We have now. Look.'

He pointed at the little screen. I leaned in close. Then I went pale with horror too. I must have done, because my stomach did a somersault and the rest of my insides did much the same. My entire body felt like an athletics meeting!

On the screen, the photo had been brightened, and sharpened, and twisted slightly. All the faces in it were now even weirder-looking than before. But the blurred one, the face of this Mr Electron person, had gained a distinct outline.

If you hadn't ever met Mr Electron in real life, you still might not have been able to tell who it was in the photo. But I *had* met him in real life. We all had.

This Mr Electron person was someone I thought I was rid of for good, someone I'd hoped I wouldn't meet again. It was my arch-enemy – that low-down rat Harry Lovecraft.

# CHAPTER
# Four

'WE NEVER DID FIND OUT which school he'd gone to, did we?' said Muddy. 'Now we know.'

(If you don't know who Harry Lovecraft is, here's a quick explanation: he's a low-down rat. If you *do* know who Harry Lovecraft is, you'll be as horrified as I was. That villainous worm, whose underhand schemes I'd foiled many times, had left St Egbert's after the events of my case file *Five Seconds to Doomsday*. I really thought we'd seen the last of him. I should have known better!)

I could hardly believe my eyes. No, on second thoughts, my eyes were telling me what I should already have guessed.

'Of *course*!' I cried, slapping a hand to my forehead. 'This case has got Harry Lovecraft written all over it!'

'But there's just this Mr Electron nickname here,' said Muddy, examining Izzy's printout.

'Noooo,' I said. 'I mean this sort of cheating is typical of what that low-down rat gets up to.' I slapped a hand to my forehead again. 'Of *course*! *That's* the reason the Spykeside team are using nicknames. *That's* the reason they want to stay anonymous. *That's* the reason Harry moved as this photo was being taken, so his face would be obscured.'

'What reason is that, then?' asked Muddy.

'Every team knows which other schools are in the competition, right?' I said. 'It's been posted up on the Brain Boom Schools Quiz Challenge website from the start. So Harry *knew* a team from St Egbert's – his old school – were taking part. He knew that if we realised he was one of the Spykeside team, we'd smell a low-down rat *instantly*.

'So he made sure that the identities of all four Spykeside team members were as hidden as possible, just so *we* wouldn't know he was involved until it was too late. Of *course*!' I nearly slapped a hand to my forehead again. But I didn't. It was giving me a headache. '*That's* why Mr Electron hasn't answered one question so far! Harry knew we'd be listening in. He didn't want to run the risk of us recognising his voice!'

'I don't get it, said Muddy. 'Surely he realised we'd be

165

on to him eventually? What if St Egbert's had been drawn to play Spykeside in round one?'

'If Harry's been able to get the questions in advance,' I said, 'he may also have been able to influence who's played who. It may be that he's rigged the competition so that St Egbert's wouldn't have any contact at all with Spykeside, unless St Egbert's also reached the grand final.'

'Which we have,' said Muddy.

'Which we have,' I agreed.

'So, he's been banking on our team not making it to the final. *Or* making it through, turning up for the final, and only *then* realising that he's been involved all along?'

'Absolutely right,' I said. 'And at that point, it'd be too late. The final would be about to happen, live on Vibe FM. We wouldn't have time to gather any proof. If we started saying "Ooooh, we know that kid and he's not to be trusted", it'd simply sound like sour grapes. He's gambled that his identity would stay hidden from us long enough for Spykeside's cheating to go unsuspected.'

'But his gamble hasn't paid off,' said Muddy. 'We've rumbled him one day early. Today's Friday, and the final is tomorrow afternoon. We've got time to go to Vibe FM and blow Spykeside out of the water.'

I thought carefully for a few moments. 'No. We shouldn't do that.'

'Huh?' gasped Muddy. 'Why? Let's go!'

'We still don't know *how* Spykeside have set this up. We don't know if Harry's got someone working for him at the radio station. If we go charging into Vibe FM, we might alert Harry's helper and the whole scheme might be shredded and covered up before we can expose what Spykeside have been up to.'

'But surely the whole questions-answered-early thing proves Spykeside have been cheating?' said Muddy. 'What more do we need?'

'We need to know exactly what this is all about,' I said. 'We need to know who is involved, and how, and why. *Is* it just about winning the prizes? *Could* there be more to this than we've seen so far?'

'I think you're being too cautious,' said Muddy. 'If Harry Lovecraft is mixed up in this, that's all I need to know. Let's get the so-and-so. We don't have much time!'

I was still wary of rushing things. I persuaded Muddy to come with me back to Izzy's house. I wanted to find out if she'd uncovered any more information. Luckily, Izzy agreed with me.

'I hate to say it, guys,' she said, spinning slowly in her glittery swivel chair, 'but it could still be the case that Harry is innocent. What if someone at Vibe FM is the real villain and is controlling the Spykeside team for some reason we don't know about yet?'

'Rubbish,' said Muddy. 'Once a low-down rat, always a low-down rat.'

'I have been wrong about Harry Lovecraft in the past,' I said reluctantly. 'Well, once anyway.'

The three of us sat there for a while, staring at each other blankly. Then we stared blankly at each other for a bit longer, because we still didn't know what to do.

At last, Izzy broke the silence. 'I have an idea,' she said. 'It's a long shot, but it might provide a few answers.'

'And your idea is . . .?' I said.

'We call Mike O'Phone,' said Izzy.

'*Who?*' said Muddy and I together.

'The DJ at Vibe FM who's the quizmaster,' replied Izzy. 'I told you before, he's probably the one who's compiling the questions. We know Harry's team is getting the questions in advance. See the connection? We call, tell him we're from Spykeside, have a little conversation, no?'

'Mike *what*?' spluttered Muddy. 'That *can't* be his real name.'

'You think?' I said, giving him a boggle-eyed look. I turned back to Izzy. 'Are you suggesting that we should ring up this DJ and pretend to be Harry Lovecraft? Are you suggesting we risk this entire investigation? Are you suggesting we resort to the sort of sneaky tactics Harry Lovecraft might use?'

'Yes.'

'Brilliant idea,' I said. 'Hand me the phone.'

A few minutes' search on the internet got us the number for Vibe FM. My fingers shook as I tapped at Izzy's mobile.

'Vibe FM, howcanIhelpyoooo?' crackled a squeaky voice at the other end of the line.

'Hello,' I said, trying not to let my voice sound wobbly. 'Can I speak to Mike O'Phone please?'

'One moment please, I'll see if he's still in the studio, who shall I say is calliiiiing?'

'Er, tell him it's Harry.'

'One moment.' There was a click and a bouncy pop tune cut in. As I waited, I glanced up at Izzy and Muddy. They looked as scared as I felt. Ten seconds later, there was another click.

'Yes? H-Harry?' said a man's voice.

My heart hopped a couple of beats. 'Mike,' I said. 'I'm calling about tomorrow's questions.' I gave myself a mental pat on the back. I could do a pretty good imitation of that low-down rat's slimy tones.

'Y-You OK?' asked Mike O'Phone. 'You sound funny. Do you have a cold?'

'Er, yes. Bad cold,' I said. 'All bunged up. Now, those questions . . .'

'I-I-I emailed them y-yesterday! Honest, I did! Like I

promised! I swear! P-Please, Harry, I sent them to the usual address, like you told me!'

'I'm, umm, on a geography field trip. Send them to my webmail, which is . . .' I snapped my fingers and pointed to Izzy's computer. She quickly scribbled down an email address for me. '. . . izzy@girliespace.net.uk.'

'. . . That's your webmail, is it?'

'Just do it!'

'Y-Yes, Harry. S-Sorry. I'll do it now.'

I switched the phone off. I let out a long breath. 'Well,' I said, 'that guy is terrified of Harry. I think we've got our answers.'

'Harry must have some sort of hold over him,' said Muddy. 'You see, I was right!'

A few seconds later, there was a bleep at Izzy's computer. A couple of mouse clicks and a handful of sheets hummed from the printer.

Izzy swung around in her chair, her eyes tightly shut. 'If those are tomorrow's questions, *don't let me see them!* We've got all the proof we need. Vibe FM's email address will be printed at the top.'

'Yeah, and so is yours,' said Muddy.

Izzy's eyes snapped open. 'Oh bum, you're right. I'm going to have to resign from the team. Someone else will have to take my place.'

'Hang on, hang on,' I said. 'There's no point worrying

about that. Harry's already got these questions anyway.'

'Yes,' said Muddy. 'And now we've all got them. It's a fair competition again.'

'Don't be daft!' I said. 'You can't have both sides cheating, it's, er, it's double cheating . . . or something . . .'

'But we can now beat Spykeside at their own game,' said Muddy.

'No way,' said Izzy. 'If the St Egbert's team take advantage of this, it'll make us as bad as them! In any case, if all the contestants know all the questions, it'll end up as a mad buzzer free-for-all! The final will have to be scrapped. I vote we take these questions to the Head, and show her what's been going on.'

'I've got a better idea,' I said with a smile. 'I've thought of a way we can stop Spykeside from winning this competition and avoid turning our own team into cheats at the same time.'

'How?' asked Muddy.

# CHAPTER
## Five

THE MAIN HALL AT SCHOOL was packed with pupils, teachers and parents, huddled on rows of plastic chairs that the school caretaker had spent all morning setting out. In front of them was a straight line of tables, with the four members of the St Egbert's quiz team (including Jeremy Sweetly and Izzy) at one end, and the four members of the Spykeside team at the other. Cables from buzzers and microphones snaked about, connecting up to a set of machines over which was crouched a Vibe FM technician.

The short, tubby shape of Mike O'Phone sat between the two teams. He had a fountain-like hairdo which was far too big for his tiny face, and a multi-coloured Hawaiian shirt which made me wish I'd worn sunglasses. He kept waving at different people, aiming a finger-gun and a snappy grin at them. Nobody took the slightest notice. Some sheets of paper were clutched in his hands.

A young woman wearing a huge Vibe FM T-shirt and a pair of headphones was fussing up and down the hall. 'Two minutes to transmission, everyone!' she shouted. 'Stand by, Mike!'

I was sitting at one end of the front row, a few seats along from the Head, who was beaming with pride and joy at the St Egbert's team. Beside me, slouched on the floor, was Jeremy Sweetly's vast, slobbery dog, Humphrey. He kept licking his chops and shedding hair all over the place. That mutt could set off my allergies at any moment! If he hadn't been a vital part of Operation: Revenge on Spykeside, I wouldn't have gone anywhere near him. I hate that dog.

Izzy and the rest of the team were looking calm and confident. At the other end of the tables, Harry Lovecraft was looking as slimy as a wet toad. I gave him a look that said, 'Oh, gee whizz, what a surprise, fancy seeing you here'. He gave me a look which said 'You can't stop me this time, ha ha ha'.

The other three members of the Spykeside team were even more horrific in real life than they'd been in that photo. Captain Cool and Superguy should have been called Creature from the Swamp and Creature from the Even Worse Swamp. It was only when the Brainiator – the one who appeared to eat nails for breakfast – stood up and went to the loo that I realised it was a *girl*!

'One minute to transmission!' shouted the Vibe FM woman.

I looked over at Izzy. She gave a faint nod.

Begin Operation: Revenge on Spykeside, Phase One.

I unhooked Humphrey's leash.

Mike O'Phone cleared his throat and shuffled his papers. He glanced over at Harry Lovecraft nervously.

'Your, umm, cold better today?' he asked.

'My what?' sneered Harry.

Jeremy Sweetly gave a little cough. Humphrey suddenly bounded over the tables and landed heavily in Mike O'Phone's lap. With a wailing cry, he toppled backwards, papers flying out of his hands in a fluttering shower.

Everyone in the hall gasped. Jeremy and Izzy hurried over to help him up. Izzy quickly gathered the papers and handed them back.

'I'm *so* sorry,' said Jeremy. 'He's a big fan of yours.'

'Oh, is he?' said Mike O'Phone. He'd been about to explode with anger, but not any more.

'Oh yes, he *loves* your show,' said Jeremy.

Mike O'Phone fired a quick finger-gun and a wink at Humphrey.

'Get that dog away!' squealed the Vibe FM woman. 'Ten seconds to transmission! Lots of applause, everyone, lots of cheers!'

Everyone started to cheer and applaud.

'Naughty doggie,' said Jeremy, ushering Humphrey back to me. 'Bad Humphrey-Wumphrey, stay there.'

Humphrey settled down next to me again. As he did so, a horrible smell suddenly drifted off him. I pinched my nose. The Head sniffed and gave me a filthy look. I hate that dog.

'Hello, hello, hello,' announced Mike O'Phone into his microphone, with a grin like a motorway of teeth running from ear to ear. 'You're listening to Vibe FM and this is the grand final of the Brain Boom Schools Quiz Challenge . . .'

The Vibe FM lady waved her hands for more cheers, and everyone cheered again.

'Both teams are ready and waiting. Are you nervous, St Egbert's?'

'We're quietly confident,' said Izzy into her microphone.

'OooKaay, are you feeling confident too, Spykeside?'

'Oh yeah,' grunted the Brainiator with a smile.

'OooKaay, we all know the rules, first to the buzzer is first to answer, two points for a correct answer, one point deducted for a wrong answer. In just half an hour, we'll know which team will be our Brain Boom champion!'

More cheering. I think everyone was getting a bit fed up of the whole cheering thing now. There was a definite feeling of Get On With It in the hall.

'Here we go!' cried Mike O'Phone. 'Fingers on buzzers! What is twelve times twenty-four?'

*Buzz!* (Spykeside.)

'Yes, Captain Cool?' said Mike O'Phone.

'Three hundred!' said Captain Cool.

Mike O'Phone's grin vanished. He re-checked his question sheets. 'Er, no, umm, that's incorrect Spykeside. One point deducted.'

The Spykeside team looked at each other, puzzled.

'OooKaay, so let's offer that question to St Egbert's. What is twelve times twenty-four?'

Izzy, Jeremy and the others sat there with hmm-dunno expressions on their faces. For several seconds there was silence. The Head gaped at the team in shock. She knew that a question like that was easy-peasy for a brainbox like Izzy. But nope, the St Egbert's team shook their heads sadly, sorry, no idea, no answer.

'Er, OooKaay,' said Mike O'Phone at last, 'the answer is two hundred and eighty-eight. Next question. The Battle of Hastings in 1066 was won by —'

*Buzz!* (Spykeside again.)

'Superguy, Spykeside?' called Mike O'Phone.

'William the Conqueror,' piped up Superguy.

Mike O'Phone squirmed slightly. 'No, you buzzed too soon there, Spykeside. Here's the full question for St Egbert's. The Battle of Hastings in 1066 was won by William of Normandy, but who did he defeat?'

Silence from the St Egbert's team. Hmm, tricky, dunno, tough one. The Head stared at them in disbelief – oh come *on*, you know that one, I *know* you know that one!

'No?' said Mike O'Phone, not quite understanding what the problem was. 'The answer is King Harold. Here we go again. In the game of snooker, what colour is the ball that's worth *six* points?'

*Buzz!* (Guess who.)

'Black!'

'Wrong.'

I was *really* enjoying this quiz. Although the Head clearly wasn't. And neither was Mike O'Phone. And neither was Harry Lovecraft.

By now, you may have spotted what my idea had been, the one mentioned at the end of the last chapter?

We'd taken the questions and changed them. Just a little bit. We'd changed, 'What is twelve times twenty-*five*?' to 'What is twelve times twenty-*four*?'; we'd changed 'The Battle of Hastings in 1066 was won by which invader?' to 'The Battle of Hastings in 1066 was won by William of Normandy, but who did he defeat?'; we'd changed 'In the game of snooker, what colour is the ball that's worth *seven* points?' to 'In the game of snooker, what colour is the ball that's worth *six* points?'

And so on, and so on. You get the idea.

We'd changed things just enough for Spykeside not to realise they'd learned all the wrong answers. Not until it was too late, anyway.

Naturally, the St Egbert's team mustn't answer any questions correctly, because they'd come up with the slightly changed versions in the first place! Now that *would* have been cheating! No, Izzy's team had to stay silent and pretend to know . . . nothing about anything.

And how had we swapped the correct questions for our own 'adjusted' ones? Look back at the disturbance Humphrey caused. Wasn't that helpful of Izzy to, er, a-hem, 'tidy up' Mr O'Phone's papers for him?

After about fifteen minutes or so, the quiz took a break for commercials. Spykeside had charged ahead, answering everything as they'd learned it. St Egbert's had been, hmm, oh dear, completely unable to even guess at a single answer.

Score: St Egbert's – zero, Spykeside – minus twenty-six.

During the break, there was a lot of what's-going-on chatter amongst the parents and teachers. The Head's state of horror and bewilderment had been getting steadily worse and she was now looking almost as weird as the members of the Spykeside team.

Harry Lovecraft and his cronies couldn't work out what had gone wrong. They kept throwing evil looks at Mike O'Phone, obviously thinking that he'd stitched them up and was trying to make them lose.

Mike O'Phone couldn't work out what had gone wrong either. He was sweating so much that the Vibe FM woman had to fetch him a towel. The look of panic on his face was shouting out three things, loud and clear:

1. Am I going barmy? I don't remember setting these questions quite like this!

2. What's Harry Lovecraft playing at? I thought they wanted to win?

3. My career as a radio quizmaster is in ruins! No correct answers, one team silent and the other team looking as useless as a cardboard frying pan!

A couple of minutes later, the adverts finished and Mike O'Phone tried (in vain) to return his grin to normal.

'OooKaay, welcome back to the grand final of the

Brain Boom Schools Quiz Challenge, where the scores are . . . a little disappointing. Let's step it up, eh, guys? Here we go, straight in with the next question. Sound waves are calculated in what unit of measurement?'

*Buzz!* (Spykeside.)

'Metres!' cried Captain Cool.

'NOOO!'

Harry slapped Captain Cool on the back of the head. Captain Cool slapped him back.

'St Egbert's?' wailed Mike O'Phone. 'Any thoughts on that one? . . . No? . . . No thoughts at all? . . . No? . . . OooKaay . . .'

Izzy, Jeremy and the others were struggling not to giggle. The Head was struggling not to shout out the answers herself. Mike O'Phone was struggling not to scream.

Spykeside tried a new tactic. They'd realised that St Egbert's wouldn't press their buzzer, so after every question they sat there, muttering, trying to agree on the *correct* answer. There were long silences, during which Mike O'Phone gibbered nervously.

Even Harry started answering questions! He got several right, but nowhere near enough to erase Spykeside's sub-zero points total. And pretty soon: 'Ten seconds to go! Teams, here's your final question. What nineteenth-century novel by the Victorian writer

Charles Dickens features a character called —?'

*Buzz!* (Superguy, Spykeside.)

'Bart Simpson!'

'*No! No! No!*' blubbed Mike O'Phone. 'Oh, for goodness' sake, *no!*'

Harry Lovecraft jabbed Superguy in the ear. Superguy flicked Harry Lovecraft's nose.

*BOOOONGGG!*

'OooKaay, the sound of the gong means time's up. That's the end of the contest, let's look at the scores. No, let's not look at the scores.'

Score: St Egbert's – zero, Spykeside – minus twelve.

'St Egbert's have won,' wailed Mike O'Phone. 'I don't know how, but they've won. I give up! I quit! Ladies and gents, listeners, kids, I can stand it no more! I can't bear the guilt! I gave Spykeside the answers! There, I said it! That boy there was blackmailing me! He found out I secretly collect Happy Bunnybears merchandise! But I don't care any more! Tell the world! Tell my mates down at the pub! I've had enough! It's the Bunnybears I love, not this rotten quiz!'

He burst into tears and the Vibe FM woman led him away, her arm cuddled around his shoulders. Meanwhile, Harry Lovecraft was in big trouble.

'You promised us those prizes!' growled the Brainiator. She knocked him back with a hefty shove.

Then the rest of the Spykeside team started describing, in disturbing detail, all the toilets they were going to stick his head down when they got back to school on Monday morning.

He broke free of them long enough to come staggering over to me. He bristled with anger, from his shiny hair to his shiny shoes.

'You did this, didn't you, Smart?' he sneered.

'Yes, Harry,' I said, smiling. 'Yes, I did.'

'One day, Smart, I'm going to have my revenge on you, once and for all.'

'Ready when you are,' I said casually.

Suddenly, Humphrey came bowling out and leaped up at Harry with a happy-to-see-you woof, dribble splattering everywhere. Harry fell flat on his back with a howling squeal, while Humphrey licked and slobbered all over his face.

I hate that dog, but I guess he has his uses.

Meanwhile, the Head – along with most of the teachers and parents – was busy congratulating the St Egbert's team, even though no one was quite sure what they were congratulating the team *for*. Izzy gave me a little wave, and I smiled back.

By the time I got back to my garden shed, I was feeling exhausted. It had been a long, strange day. I wrote a few comments about the case in my notebook, went back into the house and went straight to bed. It was only as I was drifting off into a peaceful sleep that I suddenly realised . . . 'Oh bottoms,' I mumbled, pulling the covers over my head. 'Still haven't done that science homework.'

Case closed.